DATE DUE

DATE DUE
9 6 94

DATE DUE
10 16 92

Four of a Kind

Four of a Kind

Patti Sherlock

Holiday House / New York

Library of Congress Cataloging-in-Publication Data
Sherlock, Patti.
Four of a kind / Patti Sherlock.
p.   cm.
Summary: Twelve-year-old Andy lives with Grandpa and dreams of
driving his two draft horses, Maggie and Tom, in a pulling contest.
ISBN 0-8234-0913-9
[1. Draft horses—Fiction.   2. Horses—Fiction.   3. Horse pulling
contests—Fiction.   4. Grandfathers—Fiction.]   I. Title.
PZ7.S54517Fo   1991   91-55038   CIP   AC
[Fic]—dc20

*This book is dedicated to my nephew, the late Bob Clark,
and his parents, Bobbette and Jack.*

ACKNOWLEDGMENTS

I would like to thank these people for their help: Wells Barney, Dell and Sheila Barney, Max and Karen Sommerville, Dr. Roger Brunt, and DeeDee Sihvonen.

Four of a Kind

CHAPTER 1

"Holy Jumped-up Moses! Ya think wood's free?"
Grandpa roared as I pushed open the front door.
"Close the door! That wind's sharp." Grandpa
always bellowed at me for causing a draft when I
came in from school. Yet, all winter he'd kept
forgetting to fix the cracked window that let in
wind a hawk could float on.

I flung my coat onto the broken TV and went
into the kitchen where Grandpa was. He was
shuffling around in slippers and dressed in a
thermal undershirt and blue coveralls.

"Ya hungry?" he barked.

"Yeah." I set my lunch pail on the metal table.

Grandpa handed me a yellow plastic cup and a
bottle of milk.

"There's bread in the icebox."

"Mom says it dries bread out to keep it in the
refrigerator."

"She's ten states away, ain't she?"

"Yeah."

"So I guess it ain't none o' her concern where I keep muh bread."

"I wish . . ." I stopped. I wished he didn't bawl me out all the time. Today of all days, I didn't want to argue with Grandpa.

I let my gaze travel over to Wellington Boyd's corral. Maggie and Tom, Mr. Boyd's Percheron horses, were standing with their ears perked, watching the school bus leave. They were waiting for me. Every day after school I went over to pet them and feed them hay.

Maggie, the mare, thumped to the end of the corral, then thumped back again. Grandpa says when a draft horse runs it just can't look pretty like a light horse. In draft horses, there's more power than grace, but that power is a kind of beauty, too, he says. Maggie kicked at her brother, Tom, then leaned over the worn fence poles until I thought they'd bust under her weight.

"Andy, your dad called today."

Worms wiggled inside my stomach. "What'd he say?"

"Said you was ta take them vitamins he sent up. Said he was sorry he missed ya."

My mouth flattened into a tight line. "Then

why'd he call when he knew I'd be at school?"

Grandpa straightened up and stared at me. "Don't look ta *me* ta explain what your dad does. Here, finish up there, we got clothes ta warsh."

I groaned, quiet enough so Grandpa didn't hear. I hated washdays. At my dad's house in Idaho Falls, you only had to throw clothes in a washer, add soap, and the machine did the rest. After the clothes were washed, you stuffed them into the dryer. I'd learned how to work the washer and dryer the year Mom went back to her family in Ohio.

But Grandpa owned a chipped and rusted old wringer machine that overflowed nearly every time we used it and flooded the bathroom linoleum with dirty water. And Grandpa's machine didn't rinse. You had to dunk the clothes in the bathroom sink, then put them one by one through the wringer. Half the time they got stuck.

Drying was even worse. Oh, it was all right in the summer, hanging clothes outside on the clothesline. But Dove Valley, Idaho, has more winter than summer. In winter, your fingers froze while hanging out the wash. Jeans stayed damp forever. Sometimes, if a storm was coming and you had to bring the wash in before it was dry, the sheets would be giant panes of ice you

could hardly wrestle through the cabin door.
Only good thing, Grandpa didn't feel bound to
wash clothes too often.

The old man was behind the times, all right.
He was a lot older than my friends' grandpas
because he'd married so late. Dad said Grandpa
had become his father about the time other men
were having grandkids. I liked that in some ways,
because he had been a young man in the real
old-fashioned days and knew how to do stuff like
plow with horses.

I pawed through my two suitcases looking for
dirty clothes. For the first eleven years of my life,
my clothes had lived, neatly folded, in a dresser
drawer. But when Dad decided he couldn't raise
me by himself anymore, he'd brought me up to
Dove Valley. I didn't have a dresser at Grandpa's,
and during the year I'd lived with him, my clothes
had gone from clothesline to suitcases to the
floor. Every so often, Grandpa growled at me to
clean up my room. Then I stuffed the clothes
back in the suitcases, dirty and clean together. It
would have slayed my dad, who was real tidy, to
see how I lived at Grandpa's. But Dad worked
long hours. He didn't make it up to Dove Valley
often.

Grandpa was bent over, plugging in the

washer, when I brought an armload of clothes into the bathroom. I cleared my throat.

"Grandpa, Bobby Hodges says Wellington Boyd is getting ready to sell his Percherons."

Grandpa looked at me—sharp. Then he growled, "Good idee! Ole fool, on a pension, like me, tryin' ta feed two big horses."

"Bobby says Mr. Boyd's moving to a retirement place in Arizona 'cause he can't stand another winter here. He's selling everything—the wagon and harnesses and all."

"Don't that beat all?" Grandpa muttered. "Ever'thin's changin' around here. First your grandma ups and dies, then Wellington's wife follows suit. Now old Wellington decides he's gittin' old and soft. Am I gonna be the last o' the old-timers on this road?"

"Who do you think will buy Maggie and Tom?" I cracked my knuckles to cover the crack in my voice.

"Whoever's got the money."

"Think they'll go for much?"

"Horse prices is down, in general. But Old Boyd, he thinks ever'thin' he's got is plumb valuable. He thinks draft horses is makin' a comeback."

"You think you might buy 'em?"

"Me? Land Awmighty! I may be a ole fool, but I ain't clean off muh rockers."

"You always said you wanted another team."

"I awwus wanted a warshin' machine 'at worked, too. But it don't look like I got one."

"Are you saying . . ." My voice scraped against my dry throat.

"Ain't it plain? I'm sayin' no danged fool horses! Shoot, is this worthless warsher busted? Ya been fiddlin' with it?"

I glared at his hunched-over back. What was wrong with him? Old Man Boyd's Percherons were for sale! Grandpa loved draft horses, those two especially. It was Grandpa who'd gotten me interested in big horses in the first place. Ever since I was little, he'd been taking me to the Draft Horse Pulling Contest at the Eastern Idaho State Fair in Blackfoot. He'd walk me around and point out which horses he thought would be "keen." He explained the rules to me, how the horses had to pull a stoneboat, a wagon on sled runners that the pioneers used for hauling stones, a length of ten feet. The load was increased by 500 to 1,000 pounds each try, and each time a team completed a pull, a red flag fell. During the pulling, he'd holler and cuss and squeeze my shoulders till they hurt.

And tell me how, a long time before, he'd owned a team that could pull the soda out of a biscuit.

Once, when I was about seven, Grandpa and I watched a contest where two mighty horses pulled a huge load. When the owner circled the arena to claim his trophy, everyone in the bleachers jumped to their feet and yelled. I made a promise to myself that day. Someday I'd drive a team like that and people would stand up and cheer for me.

Then, four years ago, when Wellington Boyd's big Percheron mare gave birth to twin foals, I'd added something important to my dream. The team I'd take to the fair would be those twins. Mr. Boyd had even let me name them—Maggie and Tom.

"Here!" Grandpa was kneeling on the linoleum, staring up into the washer. "Your eyes is better'n mine. Look up there and see if ya kin tell what's wrong."

Grandpa understood dogs and insects and weather better than anyone else. But he didn't understand machines. If he had, he would've known there was nothing for me to see when I crawled under the washer. Its workings were hidden inside a faded drum.

"I'll miss Maggie and Tom," I called out. My words echoed against the galvanized sides.

"Course ya will!" Grandpa squatted beside the machine. "Hadn'ta been fer you, that Tom colt wouldn'ta lived a week. Old Man Boyd shoulda give 'em ta ya. Course, with ya livin' in town, it mighta seemed impractical. Then, too, Wellington's tighter'n a boot. What d'ya see up there? Kin ya tell what's wrong?"

"There's nothing to see."

There was nothing but a metal drum. But as I gazed at it, my mind filled up with a picture. I saw a windy day, four years earlier. I saw Wellington Boyd's ramshackle barn, a straw-covered floor, and on it, two thundercloud-colored foals. It came back to me, fresh as fish on a campfire—that first time I'd ever laid eyes on Maggie and Tom.

CHAPTER 2

The morning Maggie and Tom were born, I'd just arrived at Grandpa's. Mom and Dad were going on a three-week trip and I was to stay with Grandpa in Dove Valley. I was eight years old.

No sooner had Mom carried in my suitcases and kissed me good-bye than Grandpa had called, "C'mon! Old Man Boyd's Sally was in labor early today—let's go see what she done."

I knew Old Man Boyd's draft horse named Sally was expecting a foal. Mr. Boyd had bragged about it for months. He'd bought the big Percheron mare, already bred to a fancy stud, back East someplace, like Iowa. Mr. Boyd had trailered her to Idaho as carefully as he could. He was scared the long trip might cause her to slip that expensive foal she was carrying. But she wasn't home long before she started to swell, and Old Man Boyd got so excited he talked of nothing else.

But when Grandpa and I arrived at his barn that morning, Old Man Boyd was in a rage.

"Come in here, Eldro Pendrey, and look what this hussy done ta me!" he shouted to Grandpa. *"She had TWINS!"*

I peered over the stall door. Sure enough. There were two wet, shivering black foals.

"How come he's mad, Grandpa?" I whispered. "He got two baby horses instead of one."

"Twins ain't worth a trip ta the dime store," Grandpa muttered. "They're sickly and scrawny. Anyone 'ud rather have one good one than two weak little ones."

The foals didn't look too small to me, but then, I'd never seen newborn horses before. The big mare Sally was licking one and she had a far-off look in her eyes, like she was in a happy dream. She didn't seem bothered by how she was getting cussed.

"The *trouble* I went ta! Grainin' her, exercisin' her, even in nasty weather. And *look* what she done ta me!" He shook his pudgy fist.

"Wellington, look." Grandpa nodded toward the foals. "That mare's only claimin' one of 'em."

Old Boyd stopped fuming and turned to glower at the mare. He watched her for a moment. "Looks like. The little one's just as wet as when it was born. And if she don't clean it up, she won't raise it."

"Pull the bigger one's leg up and see what it is. The face looks like she's a filly. The little one, I think it's a horse colt."

Old Man Boyd pushed Sally away and hoisted the cleaned-up foal's leg. Sure enough, it was a girl. Grandpa claimed his eyes were bad, but he could tell a whole lot of things at a glance.

Wellington Boyd rubbed his hands together and his blue bulb nose quivered. Young as I was, I understood how disappointed he must be. He'd wanted a good horse colt, to make into a gelding, to harness with his Sally mare for a pulling team.

"Want ta tie 'er up and force 'er to take 'im?"

Mr. Boyd studied on that. Then he shrugged. "Don't see why. She won't have enough milk for two. Let the runt die."

"Wellington, you're a fool!" Now it was Grandpa who was mad. *"I'd expect a jugheaded ole mare not ta know what to do with twins. But I gave you credit fer a thimble o' sense. Ya got twins, Wellington, and ya gotta make the best of it and try ta raise 'em both!"*

Old Man Boyd would yell back now, and it scared me pale when those old men thundered at each other. I cringed.

"How ya suggest I do that, Eldro? Suckle it myself?

I got a sick wife in the house—ya expect me ta tend her and that skinny rat colt, too?"

"When you're mad, Wellington, ya don't figger straight. I don't mean YOU have to tend it. Just git someone who will." He turned toward me. "Like muh grandson Andy, here. He's gonna be up here three weeks. In that time he could get 'at colt off ta a good start. It'd be good fer Andy, too. He ain't never even had a dog. Linden thinks they leave hairs on the rug."

"How'd a boy of yours end up likin' things fancy?"

"Somepin' went wrong, I figger."

My ears ached from listening so hard. What Grandpa proposed was just what I had in mind, but I never would've been brave enough to suggest it.

"Whatever ya wanna do with the fool thing," Mr. Boyd shrugged. "But warn 'im, Eldro, he ain't likely ta save 'im. Ya know how hard it is to raise a foal, and this one is puny ta start with and don't look like he's got much heart to 'im."

Old Man Boyd clumped out of the barn. Grandpa whirled on me. "Don't just stand there! Run ta our place and find some empty pop bottles. Warsh 'em out good! In the shed, there's old rubber calf nipples. Git 'em an' bring 'em!

"I'll tie up this mare and milk some colostrum

from 'er." He glanced at the smaller foal. "This feller ain't agonna make it without lots o' help, an' he needs it fast."

I turned and ran for Grandpa's like the devil was after me. I didn't know then what colostrum was—a mare's first milk that's rich in energy and vitamins and antibodies—but I did understand Grandpa thought it was life or death for the colt. I gathered the bottles and nipples in record time and sped back to Boyd's barn. Grandpa was standing beside the mare's hind end, stripping milk from her bag into a small black bucket.

He motioned for me to come over. He poured colostrum into my pop bottle, as carefully as if it were liquid gold, and fitted a nipple on top.

I don't think I'd ever been as excited. I'd never had any pet, except for a mouse I'd found in one of Dad's traps and nursed back to health. Now Grandpa and I were going to do for that foal what its own mama refused to. With his pocket-knife, Grandpa enlarged a hole in one nipple. Then he handed me the bottle.

"Good luck."

"Thank . . ." I stopped. Grandpa was swaying toward the barn door.

"Hey! Where're you going?"

"Home," he called over his shoulder.

"Don't leave me here alone!" I pleaded.

Grandpa's brows knotted in anger. "There's only one way ta give a colt a bottle," he snapped. "You figger it out."

I hauled myself up on the splintery stall door and watched him go. My mouth hung open. He'd really done it—run out on me—after setting me up for a job Old Man Boyd thought impossible.

Warily, I turned and looked at the mare. How did I know she would stay uninterested in her second foal? What if, when she saw me messing with it, she decided to rear up and trample me to death? Big dogs made me nervous and here I was, trapped in a stall with a one-ton giant.

I held the bottle toward the colt. Except for its constant trembling, it did not move. I glanced at the mare and saw she'd laid her ears back and was shoving her nose toward me. I jumped onto the stall door, told her I was sorry, and stayed there, frozen. In a minute, though, she went back to loving it up with her filly foal, and I could see Grandpa was right—she didn't care much about the colt.

I knelt beside him and lifted his head onto my lap. He didn't open his eyes. His neck seemed strangely wobbly. With both hands propping up his head, I had no free hands to hold the bottle. I let the head drop back into the straw and cursed Grandpa.

But I had to do something. I turned the colt's black muzzle toward me and pulled back his lips. I tried to open his baby teeth, but they remained locked together. I shook drops of colostrum onto the gums behind his teeth. The milk ran out the other side of his mouth and onto my jeans.

"Look!" I cried. *"If you won't swallow, how can I save you?"*

The colt's neck seemed boneless—a dark rag across my knees. I yanked off the bottle's nipple and smeared some colostrum on his lips. If only he'd lick it off. His mouth lolled open.

I lifted the colt's head, pried open his mouth, and poured a gulp down his throat. The colostrum leaked out of his mouth.

"Please . . ." I pleaded. Tears ran down my face. I'd wanted to do something big and important and I didn't know how. Just then I jumped—the barn door had swung open.

Grandpa peered over the stall. He tossed a faded bath towel to me.

"The mare, she awwus licks the colt to git its blood agoin' after it's born. This one didn't have that. Take the towel and rub the dickens out o' 'im." Grandpa frowned at the colt. "Between times, try and give 'im some colostrum. And don't worry none about gettin' home fer lunch. I'll put yours in the icebox."

"Grandpa! Don't go away again." There was a catch in my voice.

"I ain't stayin'," he said at last.

I dried off the colt, gently at first. He didn't move. Grandpa had said to rub so hard I'd worry the hide might come off. I did that. It felt good for two reasons. One was, I was mad at Grandpa. The second was, the colt opened its eyes. I tried the bottle again. I placed the foal's head on my knees and gave him the bottle to suck. His lips moved briefly and he took a halfhearted swallow. I was so grateful I laughed out loud.

But that was the last suck the colt took voluntarily. The rest of that bottle I had to force down him. First I'd rub him with the towel until my arms ached. Then I'd force back his head so his muzzle was pointing to the roof, and I'd drizzle a little colostrum into his throat. He wouldn't swallow, so I'd rub his throat to force him to gulp.

It took forever to force-feed that small portion of colostrum. Before I'd emptied the bottle, my legs were tingling with pain. I tried to stand and they buckled under me.

When I got home, Grandpa didn't ask how the colt was. He set out a sandwich for me and watched me eat it. I wanted to make him ask, but finally I grew impatient to brag.

"I got him to take it."

"Good. Is he on 'is feet?"

"No! He's barely breathing and he's cold. I put a horse blanket over him when I left."

"Another hour, you go check 'im and give 'im another dose o' colostrum. Ya'll have ta feed 'im real often fer a while, just like a mare would."

In late afternoon Grandpa came over to check the colt.

"He's tryin' hard ta die," he said. "Fer as many hours old as he is, there oughta be some improvement." He left, but returned soon, carrying half a pop bottle of black stuff.

"Give 'im this."

"What is it?"

"Coffee and Karo syrup. The caffeine should git 'is blood agoin' and the syrup'll give 'im energy."

I had to force it down him. I thought Grandpa's mixture would yield instant results, but all it did was give him coffee jitters. The colt's heart flapped against his downy black skin, his legs jerked, and his eyes flew open, looking wild.

"Land Awmighty!" Grandpa said.

"Will he make it?"

"If ya kin keep 'im alive overnight, ya got a runnin' chance of savin' 'im. But I'll be the first ta admit, it don't look promisin'."

Grandpa said if I wanted to stay in the barn that night, he'd bring over some army blankets.

So that's what I did. I still worried about the Sally mare, so I camped outside the stall. Twice in the night I got up and fed the colt. Grandpa had left his propane lantern for me so I could warm the colostrum. In the dark stall, with the colt's head on my lap, I tried not to be scared of the wind howling in the rafters and the coldness in the colt's limbs. I remembered in books people always sang to sick children. The only song I could think of was an old cowboy tune Grandpa had taught me.

> "I ain't got no mother,
> I ain't got no mother,
> I ain't got no mother
> To mend the clothes that I wear.
>
> I'm a poor lonesome cowboy,
> I'm a poor lonesome cowboy,
> I'm a poor lonesome cowboy,
> And a long way from home."

In the gray half-light before dawn, I woke up. The barn was cold. I scrambled out of my blankets and peeked over the stall door. The colt, curled up in a black ball, lifted his head and gazed at me. I ran for home.

"Grandpa!" I yelled. "He's alive!"

*   *   *

After breakfast, Old Man Boyd came out to the barn. He looked at the twins in disgust. He spat in the straw toward the colt.

"He ain't a bit o' good," he growled.

"Grandpa says he's going to make it!"

"He ain't a bit o' good," he repeated. Then he said, "Ya got a pair o' names fer these foals?"

"Yeah. Maggie and Tom."

"Them're good names."

By the time my three weeks at Grandpa's house were up, Old Man Boyd had scarcely changed his mind about Tom. He grudgingly took over the bottle feeding, which by then was down to four times a day.

The next summer when I visited Grandpa, Old Man Boyd still was claiming Tom would always be small and weak. He liked Maggie. She was filling out and starting to resemble her dam.

During that time I worried a lot about Old Man Boyd selling Maggie and Tom. But that winter, Mr. Boyd lost his wife. After that he started spending a lot of time with the horses. He planned to breed Sally again, which made me think he'd forgiven her for having twins.

The next June though, Sally got down with colic, and before the vet from Idaho Falls could get up to Boyd's place, the mare died. I felt awful about her dying. I'd spent a lot of time with all three horses whenever I'd been at Grandpa's. Maggie and Tom were all Old Man Boyd had left—I was sure he wouldn't part with them. I never figured he'd get it in his head to move away.

"See anythin' yet?" Grandpa's voice broke in on my memories.

"No, nothing."

"Takes ya plenty long ta see nothin', don't it? Come out o' there and we'll give 'er another try."

Grandpa plugged in the washing machine and pushed the silver lever. It started to fill. Grandpa didn't smile too often, but he did then. I thought a washer that sometimes worked and sometimes didn't was dangerous and nothing to smile over. But whenever the washer decided to work after first refusing to, Grandpa took it like a personal compliment.

"Now, that's fine, ain't it?"

I nodded.

"Not a thing wrong now."

I nodded again, not meaning it. Everything was wrong. Maggie and Tom were old enough to start training for pulling, they were for sale, and if Grandpa and I bought them, I would have a team to enter at the state fair. But Grandpa had said no, and Grandpa seldom changed his mind.

CHAPTER 3

I moped around the next couple of days—moping hardest when I thought Grandpa was watching. He either didn't notice or didn't let on.

I'd been looking forward to summer for so long, thinking I'd be working with Maggie and Tom, training them to be a pulling team, and now I found myself without anything to do. The June days weighed down on me like boulders.

Saturday morning I walked down to the general store and ordered an ice-cream cone.

"An ice-cream cone?" Peggy Sundstrom scolded. "It's only eight-thirty in the morning! Didn't you and your grandpa eat breakfast?"

"Is it part of your job to find out?" I snapped. Peggy was only a year older than me, but ever since she'd gotten a big-deal job as a clerk at Pat's

General Store, she liked to act smart. I took my change and left.

I ambled home on my favorite path. Pink prairie smoke bloomed on its edges. The valley was greening up. Dove Valley, Idaho, is so green in summer it almost hurts your eyes. Barb, the waitress down at the Hereford Drive-in, says tourists always marvel at the valley's emerald color. Grandpa says it's our savage winters that make it so pretty. When plants finally come to life again, they aim to dazzle.

About a mile from home I stood on a rise and looked down at Grandpa's cabin. A shiny white sports car was parked in front of it. My dad's. My stomach tightened up. I hurried down.

"Hello, Andy." Dad was picking mud splatters off the car's gleaming door. Dad worked in nuclear research at the Idaho National Engineering Laboratory. He traveled all over the world. Mom had hoped I could stay with Dad and go to sixth grade in Idaho Falls when she left Idaho to go back to college in Ohio after the divorce. But Dad worked long hours when he wasn't traveling, and he had a two-hour bus ride every day to the desert laboratory. He'd decided I couldn't stay with him. And so I'd ended up at Grandpa's.

Dad made a lot of money, but I knew I couldn't ask him for any of it to buy horses. There were things he'd buy me, things like clothes he saw as important, but not horses.

Grandpa was leaning against the front door, scowling.

Dad said, "C'mon, we'll go for a ride." I wiped my shoes on the grass, then climbed in.

Dad turned onto the highway winding behind the valley up to the high range. He liked that road because he could demonstrate how well his car could maneuver. He usually was too absorbed in his driving for conversation. That was okay, because I often didn't have much to say either. That day, especially, I felt quiet. Of course, that day turned out to be one of the only times Dad wanted to talk.

"What do you think of this?" He pointed to a TV-like box on the floor below the dashboard.

"What is it?"

"A computer. Here, let me show you. Let's say I want to go to Casper, Wyoming. I punch the code in here . . . now . . . see? Tells me what road to take to go there, how many miles it is from my home, what points of interest and facilities are on the way. Now, look. When I switch this, it shows us the road we're on."

"Neat." I was thinking I got a better view of the road we were on by looking out the window.

"Does the one-horse Dove Valley School have computers?"

"Yeah, a few. And once we took a trip over to Sundstrom's Dairy and his whole place is computerized—the feeding, milking, everything."

"Would you like your video games? I could bring up the attachment."

"Grandpa's TV is broken."

"Figures. Anyway, I've got good news for you. I've signed you up for a computer camp. Three weeks."

"Where?"

"California."

"You taking me?"

"No, I wouldn't be able to take time off work. I'm getting a paper ready for a conference. I'll send you on the plane."

"I won't know anybody."

"You'll get acquainted. You'll have lots in common with these kids. They'll be real bright."

Hearing Dad suggest I was bright warmed me up some. But I didn't want to go. That morning I'd been thinking I had nothing to do. Now I remembered a dozen reasons why I couldn't go to a computer camp.

"Well, I'm, uh, counting on doing a lot of fishing on Dove Creek. And Bobby Hodges and I plan to play a lot of ball."

Dad scowled. "Andy, I can buy you advantages I never had. And computers are important to your future in a way fishing isn't."

"And besides I . . ." I stopped. He wouldn't understand about my wanting to see Maggie and Tom. If I stayed in Dove Valley, I could at least visit them every day till Old Man Boyd sold them.

I rubbed my palms against my jeans. "I probably shouldn't leave Grandpa alone."

"Ffffft," Dad laughed. "That solitary old badger knows how to take care of himself."

I searched my head for another excuse. Inspiration hit. What did my Dad think was really important. *Working.*

"Well, anyway," I said, "I . . . um, have a job." I spoke the words into my shirt collar.

"You do? Where?"

"Oh, uh, helping a farmer. Mr. Schwartz."

"Schwartz? I don't know him. What will you do? You're big for twelve years old, but not big enough to be useful on a farm."

"Oh, yeah," I snapped my fingers against my palm. "Mr. Smart says I'll be good help."

"Smart?" Dad looked at me questioningly. "You mean Schwartz?"

"Uh, Schwartz. Yeah. Tobias Schwartz."

Dad shifted his attention to moving around the sharp curves with, as he said, "exactness." I hoped he would forget about my summer job so I wouldn't have to make up more lies.

But when we dropped back into the valley, he asked, "What will this farmer pay you?"

"I . . . I don't know for sure yet."

"Well, don't let the old man get into your wages. I pay him adequate money to keep you."

My chest tightened and I had to stare out the window. I didn't like Dad suggesting Grandpa would try to steal money from me. And I didn't like hearing that Grandpa got paid to keep me. Like I was a boarder, instead of his grandson.

At the turnoff to the cabin, I started to get out because Dad hated to drive up the mucky road. But a wave of guilt about my lie held me back.

"Um, Dad, could you come up some Saturday and . . . um . . . go fishing or something?"

"Andy, I'll try." He gazed at me. A shadow of worry came into his eyes. "My job won't always be so hectic."

Grandpa suddenly appeared beside the car. He'd come down for the mail. I wanted to get away quick, but first thing Dad said was, "Andy tells me he has a summer job on a farm."

Grandpa bent over and peered into the window at me. I knew Grandpa. He could watch ants in July and tell what kind of a winter would follow. A guy like that can spot a lie on a kid's face easy. Grandpa studied my face, looked sidelong at Dad, then back at me.

"Well," he said, staring into my eyes, "work's good fer kids, I awwus say."

"Don't let this Schwartz take advantage of Andy, underpay him, that sort of thing."

"I'll talk to 'im myself," Grandpa said. One side of his mouth disappeared into his wrinkled cheek.

We walked along in silence. At the cabin Grandpa said, "Draw some water and throw it on the garden. Then come in and eat."

During dinner Grandpa ate his beans slowly, smacking noisily and washing down each mouthful with a drink of water. I figured I'd have to be the one to bring up my summer job.

"I told Dad I had a job because he'd signed me up for a camp I didn't want to go to."

"Why not?"

"I want to stay here." My voice cracked.

Grandpa slopped up the last of his beans with

his bread while looking hard at me. I wriggled in my chair. Couldn't he say something, like he was glad to have me?

"Anyway, I might get a job." Lots of kids my age had jobs in the valley.

"What d'ya figger ya'd do?"

"I don't know. I haven't looked around yet."

"Ya ain't never worked before. Ya might not last the summer."

"I'd last!"

"Even on a hard, sweaty job 'at makes your bones ache with tired?"

"Yeah. You think I couldn't?"

Just then a knock startled us both.

"Eldro!" It was Wellington Boyd's booming voice.

"Land Awmighty! Shut the door!" Grandpa always yelled at Old Man Boyd just like he yelled at me. Boyd clumped in.

The two old men liked to sit around evenings and drink coffee and talk. Old Man Boyd and Grandpa had been neighbors since they were young. Grandpa was the only person Boyd had left to talk to.

"Ya don't need ta run off, Andy."

I was halfway out the back door when Grandpa said that. I wanted to slip over and visit Maggie and Tom, but now I was stuck. Old Man Boyd had two topics of conversation. One was how good things used to be. The other was how hard and terrible things used to be. I slipped back into my chair, put my head down in my arms, and let my mind drift over to Boyd's corral.

"I won't mind that in Arizona there's a restaurant right next to them apartments I'm moving ta, and I'll be able ta git coffee 'at don't taste like rattler venom."

Grandpa plunked Boyd's cup in front of him. "Your waitress won't be near as good-lookin' as me."

I went on daydreaming until I heard the word *horses*.

"So you're fer sure sellin' 'em?"

"Them and the wagon and riggin' an' all!"

"Where ya figger ya'll find a buyer?"

"A man and his wife from Montana come by. He thought Mag and Tom looked too light fer a pullin' team, but she tumbled fer 'em. I reckon the wife'll win out."

I hadn't cried when Grandpa said no to buying Maggie and Tom. I was too numb, I guess. Now the truth hit me—Maggie and Tom would belong to someone else—maybe someone who lived hundreds of miles away. All of a sudden my eyes sprung tears. I looked out the window so no one would notice.

"How much ya figger they'll bring, Wellington?" Grandpa waited a moment and then added,
"Unbroke and small fer their age?"

"I told the Montana couple seven hundred dollars each."

Grandpa whistled.

"Their pedigree makes 'em worth every dime
of it! If the horse market wasn't down, I'd ask a
whole lot more. I ain't decided yet what ta ask fer
the equipment."

Grandpa settled back in his chair. He studied
on it awhile.

"Wellington, your wagon and harnesses is almost wore out. There's people like collectors 'at's
crazy about old stuff, but they never make it up ta
this country. Maybe ya oughta junk it."

Boyd frowned. "Sounds like *you* might be scout-
in' a bargain."

"I ain't. But muh grandson, he might be."

I was so startled I almost fell off my chair.

"But you said . . ."

"I said I wouldn't buy 'em. But with you gittin'
a job, it puts ever'thin' in another light."

I thought I should point out I didn't really
have a job and didn't know if I could find one.
But it seemed smarter to keep my mouth shut.

Grandpa was scowling. But his eyes held a sparkle. I remembered stories he'd told me about horse trading in the old days—how a man needed to be good at it and how other men, even those who got outfoxed, respected shrewdness. Grandpa stared at Old Man Boyd until he began to fidget.

"Well, ya heard muh price, Eldro. Same ta you as it'd be ta anyone else. That's only good business."

"Course it is!" Grandpa smacked his fist on the table. "I don't like ta see a man git mushy about 'is price. Business is business—friendship is friendship. If ya've set a fair price, stand by it! It'd be a fair price in a good year, anyway. Just 'cause three or four big-name draft-horse raisers has gone belly-up this year and throwed their stock on the market fer almost nothin' don't mean ya shouldn't stand by your price."

Grandpa scooted his chair closer. "An' don't go soft on it just 'cause it's me and muh grandson! Just 'cause Andy here done pulled that Tom colt back from death an' if it wasn't fer him ya'd only have one horse ta sell, that's no consideration here."

Grandpa held up a gnarled finger. "Some fellers set a price and then go all nostalgic. Thinkin' what the past has meant. Don't do that!

Don't start takin' inta account it was my Josie 'at
pulled your Ludeen through the flu in thirty-
five, spoonin' hot soup inta 'er day and night.
And when your boy Bud was no bigger'n Andy
here and broke 'is leg, and the snow was so bad
you couldn't git back home, Red Richards and
me drug little Bud eighteen miles on a sled ta the
doctor. *Don't* start thinkin' stuff like that when
ya're dealin' horses."

Grandpa's face was fierce. Old Man Boyd's was
tortured. I knew he wanted to be mad at
Grandpa, but the old memories were too strong.
He gazed down at the table and drew circles in its
dust.

Finally he said, "Eldro, you're right about what
kinda neighbor ya been ta me. And about how
Andy helped out good when them foals was
nothin' but a nuisance ta me. If I was ta trim muh
prices fer anyone, it'd be fer him. And you."

"Four hunnert apiece?" Grandpa put in
quickly.

"That's too low!"

"It's eight hunnert more'n ya'll have if no one
happens up here ta buy 'em. And higher'n ya'd
git at the auction sale, without the trouble o' tryin'
ta git 'em there."

"Them Montana people might be back."

"Wellington, ya know as well as I do . . . if a

person don't love a horse enough ta take it home
with 'im, or put earnest money on 'im, he never
does come back."

Boyd looked glum.

"I sure would hate ta see ya all packed up,
ready ta go ta Arizona, an' still worryin' 'bout
them horses. Ya better take a bird in the hand at
three hunnert."

"A minute ago ya said four hunnert."

"Okay, four hunnert, if that's your final offer."

"It ain't. I gotta think about it."

Boyd's face was a dark cloud as Grandpa re
filled his mug.

"Eldro," he said at last, "I think I'm lettin' ya
rob me, but okay. Four hunnert each."

Grandpa tried not to look too pleased with
himself.

"Me 'n' Andy, we're gonna haf ta talk about the
wagon. Might could, we could build ourselves
one."

Boyd waved good-bye and clumped toward the
front door. A moment later Grandpa felt a draft
and faced it angrily.

"Shut that door! You're lettin' in the wind!"

"Grandpa! Why didn't you say I could have the
horses if I got a job to pay for them?"

"Why didn't ya say ya was willin' ta git one?"

The truth was, I *wasn't* willing to. I wanted to

fish, hike, and play ball with Bobby Hodges. I didn't want a sweaty farm job, and anyway, I had no idea where I'd get one.

Grandpa seemed to read my mind. "I'll tell ya where ya kin git a job. This here one requires a man with a team o' horses. You kin train 'em ta pull while you're payin' 'em off."

"Where?"

"Broman's."

"The sheep ranch? Doing what?"

"Feedin'. Broman lost both 'is old pulling horses over the winter. He's feedin' with a tractor now, but it keeps gittin' bogged down. Ties up 'is tractor, too. Ya'd have ta start soon. Call 'im and say ya'll start on Wednesday."

When I called Dusty Broman, he said I could have the job. After I hung up, I caught Grandpa grinning.

"Better call this Schwartz feller—tell 'im ya got yourself a different job. Don't know 'im, er I'd do it fer ya."

I wanted to hug Grandpa. A job, I didn't much want. But a job driving a pulling team! . . . I wanted to buck and squeal. I was getting Maggie and Tom! I was going to sit up on a wagon, drive them around, and make money doing it!

Before going to bed, I wrote Mom a letter,

announcing that I was buying the horses. But it wasn't until I turned my light out that everything hit me full force. In four days I had to report to work with a team that knew how to pull. And Maggie and Tom hadn't even been started.

CHAPTER 4

"Git up and feed and brush them horses!"
Grandpa barked at me at 5 A.M. Sunday. "And
eat this here egg 'fore it's cold."

After breakfast I tottered, half-asleep, to the
corral. Maggie and Tom thumped to the fence to
greet me. Tom nuzzled me. "You're mine now,"
I told him. I supposed he'd never thought otherwise.

The sun was beaming when I finished brushing them both. I was beginning to wonder if
Grandpa expected me to train them without his
help, like I'd nursemaided Tom when Tom was a
runt colt. But pretty soon Grandpa came hob-
bling toward Boyd's corral. I hopped over the
fence and ran to meet him. He met my smile with
a grimace.

"Ya think them horses don't know nothin'
about pullin'?" he demanded.

"Course they don't," I answered. "They haven't had any training."

"Huh. People awwus likes ta think horses don't know nothin' but what they taught 'em theirselves. But horses kin remember plenty."

"They can't remember something they haven't learned."

"Oh they *kin't*? I say they *kin*! Not remember like *you* mean. But rememberin' what their ancestors has done." He poked his finger on my chest. "If *you* think they don't know nuthin', *they'll* think it. And that'll slow us down." He limped toward Boyd's corral, and I followed right behind. "On the other hand, ya kin't push 'em too fast neither.

"Later today, ya better start diggin' holes fer a corral. Maggie and Tom kin stay at Boyd's while he's here, but when he sells out, ya'll have ta be ready ta move 'em." Sounded to me like getting my heart's desire meant loads of work.

"Are we going to buy Boyd's wagon and equipment?"

"Ya won't need a wagon fer a while. Broman has one, and we'll use muh old collars and harnesses fer trainin'. When your job there ends, when Broman takes 'is sheep onta the forest, ya'll want a wagon o' your own. By then, Old Boyd might offer us a good deal. Here's a rope. Don't drag it in the mud! Go lead them horses around."

This was something I understood. I'd been leading them around since they were babies. I hooked the rope onto Maggie first. I'd raise more admiration leading her. She was perkier, and during the last year her dark coat had lightened to shiny gray. She was excited to see me and pranced beside me, the sun glaring off her dappled rump. She may have been small for her age by Percheron standards, but from where I stood, she looked mammoth. Despite that, I had no fear of her.

"Let 'er git the vinegar out," Grandpa said. I let out the rope so Maggie could dance around me in circles.

"Land Awmighty, she moves clean!"

"She's taller'n Tom. That's bad fer a pullin' team."

"Ain't she got a pullin' chest on 'er?"

When Maggie was done playing, I put the rope on Tom. Tom was a quieter horse—less energetic and never jumpy. But he liked to knock off your hat, nibble your jacket, and step on your toe and pretend it was an accident.

Tom chewed on the rope, tried to shove me over with his big muzzle, and searched my pockets for carrots. "Quit!" I scolded. "Go on now and get some exercise." He put on a surprised expression, perked his ears, and began to run in circles. He was shallow in build, even I could see that. He wasn't "graying"—turning the traditional dapple gray Percheron color—as fast as Mag, and was still nearly black.

"They're plumb gentle, both o' em. If they wasn't, we couldn't think about startin' 'em ta work four days from now. C'mon, bring 'em over ta Wellington's shed."

A weathered lean-to adjoined the corral and gave the horses shelter in the winter. Grandpa told me to tie Maggie to the manger inside the lean-to.

"Bring a two-by-four from our junk pile and wedge it behind 'er rump fer a barricade. I think this mare'll take ta trainin' like locusts ta the phayraoh's corn," Grandpa went on. "Let's dress 'er up and see what she thinks o' herself." He fixed his eyes on me. That meant I had to go home and fetch the collars and harnesses.

I walked home grumbling. Only 7 A.M. and I was worn out already. I came back lugging the dusty equipment and coughing. Grandpa frowned at the dry, cracking leathers.

"We'll have ta soften up this stuff with oil and replace some straps tanight. Here, hand me that collar. Not that way, that's upside down!"

He moved to Maggie's left side. "Now, ya know

ya awwus work from this side o' the horse, don't
ya?"

I nodded.

"And ya know ya awwus speak their name
when ya come up on 'em from behind?"

"Yes."

"Okay, let me slip this collar up on 'er and we'll
see how it goes." Now that Grandpa was standing
next to Maggie, he'd smoothed the cracks out of
his voice.

"Here now, Mag, no, don't jump—it ain't
agonna hurt ya. Now, when ya're plumb relaxed
in that collar, we'll put on this here contraption."

After Maggie stopped flicking her skin,
Grandpa gathered up the harness and moved to
Maggie's head.

"Andy, horses' noses is as important to them as
our five senses are ta us. If a horse kin see and
feel and smell somethin' with 'er nose, she won't
fear it no more."

Maggie smelled the harness and snorted.
Grandpa carefully laid it over her back. He
moved a distance away, not sure what the big
animal might do. She only cranked her head
around to see. After Maggie relaxed completely,
Grandpa removed the harness.

"She'll do. I knowed she would."

"Is that all for today?"

"Nope. We'll let 'er rest a minute, then do it over again."

The next time Grandpa put the harness on, he put the crupper under her tail. Maggie flinched, but otherwise was still.

"It's gonna feel funny to 'er walkin' with all this stuff on. Move that board, Andy, and I'll untie 'er."

I wondered what Grandpa would do if Maggie gave him trouble. For his age he was strong, but next to that big horse, he looked old and shrunken.

The feel of the harness did startle her. Maggie started prancing. Grandpa jerked her lead rope hard, but his voice remained soft.

"Sure, it flops and hits ya all over and feels peculiar, but don't let it scare ya."

Grandpa walked her around the corral four or five times. I noticed he squared his shoulders and seemed to limp less. When he returned, the webbing of scowl lines on his face had relaxed and a light shone from his eyes.

"Here, you try." He handed me the rope. I led Maggie around several times and then urged her into a trot. The harness slapping her back spooked her and she jumped sideways. I spoke to her and we started off again at a trot. She didn't jump again.

"We'll do one more thing with 'er today," Grandpa said. He picked up a bridle. He warmed the cold steel bit in his hands, then he withdrew something from his shirt pocket. I leaned over to look—it was a restaurant packet of honey. "Picked this up at the Hereford one day. Figgered if I wanted ta take it home, instead o' puttin' it on muh biscuits, that was my affair." He oozed a stream of honey onto the bit.

"Horses're like kids—they like sweets. Mag'll feel funny about takin' this bit at first, so we'll give 'er a little coaxin'.'"

He had to stand on an overturned toolbox to place his arm over Maggie's neck. With his free hand he eased the bit up past her chin and fastened the strap.

"Did she take it already?"

"Like a veteran. Land Awmighty! Ain't this a pleasure?" Grandpa slammed his fist against my shoulder. "Don't ya hope we do this good with the other one?"

We didn't. Tom wasn't goosey—he was even calmer than Maggie—but at every point there were setbacks. When Grandpa laid the harness across his back, Tom reached around, took hold of a strap with his teeth, and pulled the whole thing off onto the ground. Then Grandpa had to untangle it from Tom's feet. Grandpa cussed him in a whisper.

When Grandpa was drizzling honey onto the bit, Tom smacked Grandpa with his nose. The honey packet flipped upside down on Grandpa's sleeve and honey oozed over his arm and hand.

After trying Tom in the bit, Grandpa said, "C'mon, let's unhook 'im, that's enough fer to-day." Grandpa shook his head. "This geldin' is smart as a wolf. But jokers kin be plumb worth-less when it comes ta workin'.'" Tom reached over, removed Grandpa's cap with his teeth, and neatly deposited it onto a manure pile.

We were brushing down the horses when we heard a horn honk. Reed Sundstrom, who owns the dairy, waved at us from the end of the field.

"What're you doing, Eldro?" he called. "Work-ing Wellington's horses for him? Let the lazy old buzzard do his own work."

"Ain't Wellington's no more," Grandpa hol-lered back. "As o' last night, they're muh grand-son's."

Grandpa walked over to the car and Peggy Sundstrom got out and headed for me. The Sundstroms were coming from church, and Peggy wore high-heeled shoes that made her wobble. Her two little sisters were tugging on her arms.

"Careful," I said when they got near, "the horse could accidentally step on somebody."

Peggy pulled her sisters back. "It's real pretty."

Peggy and her sisters watched me brush Tom while Grandpa and their father talked beside the car. After a while, Mr. Sundstrom honked for his girls, and Grandpa limped back to me. Peggy started to leave, then hesitated. In the voice she used when she was bus monitor, she asked, "You and your grandpa always work on the Sabbath?"

I started to answer, but Grandpa moved over beside her and put his leathery face next to hers.

"What does your preacher do on a Sunday?"

"He preaches!"

"What fer?"

"To . . . um, teach people stuff."

"Well, that's just what we're adoin' here." Grandpa's voice was sweet as Karo syrup. "We're teachin', like your preacher does, so there can't be nothin' wrong with it."

Peggy couldn't see he was poking fun.

"That's different! Horses don't have *souls*." Her lips pulled into a tight little O as she collected her sisters.

I figured Grandpa was waiting until she was out of earshot to either laugh or cuss her. In-

stead, when he turned around, his face was troubled.

"You believe that, Andy?"

"What?"

"That horses ain't got souls?"

"I . . . I don't know."

"Don't never think that. 'Cause if ya do, we'd
just as well hang it up before we git inta this too
fer." He ran his hand over Tom's chest and
looked past me with watery, worried eyes. I
couldn't figure what had put him in such a sober
mind.

I walked to the shed to hunt up the posthole
digger. What did Grandpa mean, ". . . before we
git into this too fer"? Then it hit me and I had to
grin. Without saying a word to each other,
Grandpa and I had both hatched the same
scheme. Like me, the old man had set his heart
on taking Maggie and Tom to the pulling contest
at the state fair.

CHAPTER 5

Training went well. We'd moved fast, though we'd kept lessons short and stopped whenever the horses seemed tired. Grandpa said Maggie was "born broke." He got mad at Tom's pranks, but he was starting to admire him.

On our second day of training, Grandpa had put lines on Tom to drive him around the corral. Grandpa walked behind, holding the lines and carrying a whip to reinforce his git-up command if necessary. But Grandpa had no more thought *git up* than Tom perked his ears and stepped off.

As the lessons went on, Grandpa found that whenever he thought a command, Tom would obey it before Grandpa even had a chance to give him a cue.

"Dang if it ain't a nuisance ta have us a mind-readin' horse," Grandpa grumbled.

He paid Maggie the highest of compliments.

"This Maggie is as good as ole Bess was." Bess was a mare he'd owned forty years before, and she'd just about become a legend among people who'd known her. "When she was pullin', she'd git down and stretch so ya couldn't've throwed a hat under 'er."

Grandpa was quiet with the horses, but he didn't mind yelling at me.

"Only say *whoa* if ya want 'em ta stop! That's a word kin save your life—don't say *whoa* when ya mean *easy*."

"Git outa that horse's mouth! The point is ta see how *little* ya kin pull on 'em ta make 'em stop, not how *hard*!"

"Holy Jumped-up Moses! Foller through when ya give 'em a command! They ain't never gonna respect ya unless ya make 'em do what ya say!"

I would have quit if it hadn't been for one thing. Grandpa said the horses were doing great. Grandpa was tempted to harness them together for their first pulling lesson, but he argued himself out of it. "Awwus have hooked up a green horse with a doe-cile old horse fer its first lesson—so I better find me a ole plug ta borry." He remembered Ted Smith on Cinder Road had a twenty-year-old Belgian crossbred named Bill. He called Ted.

"SAY, TED, YA THINK WE COULD BORRY OLE BILL TA BREAK SOME COLTS?"

Grandpa always yelled into the telephone, and no one could persuade him it wasn't necessary. "IT DON'T MATTER HE AIN'T BEEN HITCHED UP IN YEARS, BILL'LL REMEMBER."

Next morning early, Grandpa dropped me off at Smith's. Then I led Bill the five miles home to our cabin. Grandpa had dragged out his old stoneboat. Grandpa's stoneboat was full of splinters and half the floor was rotted away; still, it would serve the purpose. Grandpa liked training horses on a stoneboat because it couldn't run up on a green horse and scare it like a wagon with wheels could. Horses competing at the fair pulled stoneboats, too.

Old Man Boyd hadn't come over to drink coffee with Grandpa since we'd bought Maggie and Tom. Grandpa said, "Guess I'll have ta swaller muh pride to go borry Old Boyd's doubletree."

I trailed behind Grandpa to Boyd's cabin. From his porch I heard Old Man Boyd holler, "Sure, Eldro, take the thing! But why didn't ya jist take it from the shed? Ya didn't mind stealin' muh horses!"

That irked Grandpa. He was cantankerous as a badger when we came home with the doubletree, the wooden bar that connects the wagon to the tugs on the harness. One good thing came of it. Old Man Boyd started dropping around to offer advice. I liked having him there. He and Grandpa were so busy trading insults, Grandpa let up on me.

First, Grandpa hooked Maggie up with Bill. Maggie looked confused, and stomped and blew. But when Grandpa said, "Git up," Maggie didn't hang back and let Bill do all the work, and she didn't charge ahead. She just pulled like she'd been pulling for years.

"Well, she pulls, but then I knowed she would!" Grandpa exclaimed.

"Some don't," Old Man Boyd muttered to me. "Jist 'cause they're draft horses don't mean they'll pull."

When Grandpa moved Tom to Bill's side, Tom laid back his ears and then piled into the old gelding. My stomach hurt as we hooked the two horses together. If Tom turned out to be too silly or lazy, it would crush all our plans. The job at Broman's would be out, the state fair would be a smashed dream. If Tom didn't turn out right, it didn't matter how good Maggie was—we'd be without a team.

"Git up," Grandpa clucked. Tom and Bill took off together. Tom pulled without crowding and he listened with ears perked for Grandpa's commands. I slumped against the fence with relief.

"He'll do," Grandpa said.

By noon we were done with Bill, and Grandpa told me to take him home. Walking the gelding back and forth for the next couple of days would mean ten miles a day. I threw the halter rope around Bill's neck for a rein, shoved him next to a fence, and climbed on him.

I'd gone riding with Bobby Hodges a few times, bouncing behind the saddle on his Appaloosa. Riding wasn't an interest of mine. Still, riding Bill back and forth would be less work than walking.

Bill was so wide my legs were stretched out of their sockets trying to straddle him. Then, when Bill could see Smith's barn come into view, his old body quivered and he started to trot. I had no bit in his mouth so I couldn't stop him. My backside smacked against his backbone. I couldn't get a good grip and I began to slide off. I grabbed him around the neck and hollered, "Whoa!"

He stopped so suddenly I fell off anyway, but I missed the pavement and rolled onto a grassy shoulder. Bill waited for me to get up. I walked him the rest of the way to Smith's. I should have felt stupid. Instead I was happy to think I'd commanded a ton of animal with only one word. After that I rode Bill both ways, but always with a bridle on him.

I hoped when I started work at Broman's, Maggie and Tom would pull the feed wagon, right off. But Grandpa decided it was smarter to hitch each of them up with Bill the first few times.

"The worst thing ya kin have with a green team is a runaway. Ya'll be feedin' in a big open area, there'll be new sounds and smells, and ya can't never tell if somethin' might scare 'em and they'll take off."

"How would I stop them if they did?"

"Stop! There ain't a man alive strong enough ta stop a runaway team, let alone a snot-nosed kid! The worst thing is, it scares the horses ta be outa control. Makes 'em run all the harder. It'd set the trainin' back months."

The morning I started work at Broman's, I got up at 4 A.M. First Grandpa and I unloaded our equipment at Broman's, then I rode Bill over, and finally, led Maggie and Tom from home. I thought once those big horses were hooked up and ready to drive, I'd be the happiest kid in five counties. But when I gazed down at those powerful rumps and the lines connecting them to Grandpa, I was too tired to care.

Dusty Broman, a sinewy man with a sun-withered face, pointed down to his haystack.

"We've got two thousand ewes with lambs here, so we're feedin' about three tons morning and night. Make a circle around the lot, droppin' the hay off in fifty-pound piles."

Grandpa touched the brim of his billed cap. "Git up," he said.

The rhythmic clink and grind of harnesses and wagon could have put me to sleep on my feet. But when we turned onto the rutted path leading down to the sheep lot, I woke up fast.

Grandpa had tightened his grip on the lines, and I noticed his few lower teeth chewed on his top lip.

"Eeeesy, Mag, Eeeeesy, Bill, Eeeeesy, Mag, Ee-eesy, Bill." He looked at me sidelong. " 'Member I said there was times ya hoped they'd remember more'n they'd ever been taught? This is one o' them times. Ain't no way ta teach a horse how ta go down a rough, steep hill except ya take 'em down it an' hope they don't spook on ya and turn the wagon over."

He talked them down every foot of the hill. When we reached the bottom, he glanced at me.

"Whew," I said.

"Whew," he answered. "Now let's go load this wagon. Trot!"

I had to grab the front bars of the wagon to avoid falling off. Grandpa, to my amazement, was standing as erect as if he were on solid ground instead of on a wagon pitching and heaving over a furrowed road.

"Stand back farther," he ordered. He was standing in the middle of the wagon, pulling back on the reins. I tried to wobble over to where he stood, but as soon as I let go of the bars, I lost my balance.

Grandpa chuckled. "Git down and open that gate fer us."

When I climbed back on the wagon, Grandpa handed me the reins. "Git up," he called to the horses. They pranced off, and I fell over and slid down the splintery boards to the wagon's edge. Grandpa, grinning, grabbed the lines.

He stopped the wagon by the haystack. "Throw them bales on now!" he hollered to me. To Maggie he cooed, "Now, no need ta jump ever' time a bale hits."

At first it was fun. But after a few minutes I had to take off my jacket. A few more minutes and I pulled off my shirt. The morning was cool, but sweat ran into my eyes, making it hard to see. Grandpa handed me his ragged blue handkerchief to tie around my forehead.

The old man was always taking on about how

soft modern kids were, so I tried to hide my heavy breathing. But my back began to ache and my arms were trembling with fatigue. When finally Grandpa drove off with the wagon loaded, I stretched out on top of the haystacks.

I forked off the hay as Grandpa drove. Hundreds of recently shorn ewes crowded up behind the wagon. The blatting of lambs caused a terrible racket. The sheep made Maggie watchful and jumpy. Grandpa stopped the wagon and let her take a long look at them.

When we finished, Grandpa showed me the stalls in the barn where Maggie and Tom would stay.

"Ya're bein' paid by the hour, so when ya finish each time, hurry and unhitch so Broman won't regret hirin' ya. Hang them harnesses here. Hurry! *Not sa fast!* Wipe the sweat off them straps!"

That afternoon, we hitched Tom up with Bill. And Grandpa surprised me. As we started down the rutted, steep hill, he handed me the reins.

"That horse knows I don't trust 'im. But *you* do."

I was flattered. And also surprised at how much calmer I felt as the teamster than I had as the passenger. I guess I was so busy trying to keep Tom calm, I couldn't let myself be edgy.

Tom behaved as sensibly as Maggie. And instead of being frightened by the sheep, he seemed to like them, and perked his ears each time one came into view. I think if he hadn't been restrained by a harness and wagon, he would have joined the lambs bouncing around the meadow.

Of course, the afternoon feeding meant loading three more tons of hay. By the time we unhitched, I was numb. Grandpa, on the other hand, was talkative as a pocket gopher all the way home.

"Ya ever think the first day with a pair o' colts 'ud go sa good? I think we got ourselves a team! Ever tell ya about the time—I was 'bout your age—Pa got a winter freightin' contract? We had ta bring supplies over the mountain inta Dove Valley on a sled . . ."

At home he scurried around the kitchen, fixing a real dinner. We usually ate canned foods, along with a few raw vegetables from our garden. But that night Grandpa set on the table two plates heaped with lamb chops, baked potatoes, cooked green beans, and biscuits.

"Don't look like that!" he growled. "Yeah, I know how ta cook. Awwus did muh own cookin' till I married Josie. Then I got spoilt. Ya gonna eat it er just stare at it? Workin' men needs ta eat!"

After dinner I meant to show Grandpa I appreciated it by washing up the dishes. But when I sat down on the couch to take off my boots and socks, I leaned my head back and fell asleep. Grandpa must have covered me with blankets, because I was sleeping warm in that same spot when he woke me next morning.

"I let ya sleep in 'cause we ain't got as much messin' around ta do this mornin'," he grunted. "Come git your oatmeal." I opened an eye and looked at the clock. It was 5 A.M. I ached too much to move. But Grandpa, already dressed in his jacket and cap, rocked on his heels beside the front door. Groaning, I hauled myself up.

CHAPTER 6

"Hey! Wait up!"

I was walking home from Pat's General Store when Bobby Hodges hollered to me.

"Where've you been all summer? I've been over, but nobody's ever home." He pointed to the fishing rod tied on his bike. "Wanna go?"

"I can't. Grandpa and I have to be back at Broman's in an hour for the afternoon feeding."

"Gol', you're lucky to have a job like that. I'm movin' irrigation pipe this summer. Kid that works over at Forbes's farm said he almost picked up a rattler the other day, wound around a pipe."

"Hodges! It's too high up here for rattlers. Have a peanut."

"How long you going to be working for Broman?"

"He's taking his sheep up to graze the forest on the Fourth of July. I have to find another job

then, Grandpa says, to help pay off the horses
and buy next winter's feed. Maybe I can move
pipe."

"You'll think it's a drag, after the job you got
now."

"You think my job's fun? Loading six tons of
hay a day? The first few days my back and arms
hurt so much I couldn't sleep at night. Now I just
hurt all the time. I get up at five A.M. every day.
I always have itchy hay down my neck. I draw
every hornet in the valley 'cause I'm so sweaty,
and I got three stings on my arms."

"Is it fun to drive a team?"

"Yeah! Except for the stupid baby lambs—they
get in the path and won't move—just stare at
you."

"Like this." Bobby made a dumb lamb face. I
laughed. Some kids, especially girls, said Bobby
was funny-looking, but I thought he had the
greatest face in the world. He could scrunch it up
and make it look like anyone or anything. He
could slick back his hair and set his jaw a certain
way and look just like the president. Our teacher
told Bobby it was disrespectful, but the school
librarian used to whoop and laugh every time
Bobby pulled that face.

"And," I went on, "if you think it's not tricky to

try to fork hay off the wagon and drive at the same time, you're wrong."

"I thought Grandpa Grumpo was helping you." Bobby made a bird face that resembled Grandpa.

"He has been. But tomorrow I start working alone."

"You going home at all this summer?"

"No. Why?"

"Just wondered. Must be lots of neat things to do in town. Arcades, movies 'n' stuff."

"I like it here. Anyway, I can't go home 'cause Dad's working on a big project and he's not home much. He's going to Washington, D.C., for a month, then to Germany at the end of the summer."

"Gol', he must be important. Nobody ever sends my folks on a trip. They're always at home, keepin' an eagle eye on us kids."

"That's not so bad."

Bobby wrinkled his forehead.

"I mean, that's what parents are supposed to do," I said. "Be around."

Bobby shook his head. After a minute he asked, "What time you get through today?"

"About six."

"Let's go fishing."

*   *   *

Next morning when I came outside, Grandpa
was already in the pickup, revving up its hoarse
old engine. He was singing and his voice was as
raucous as the engine's.

"I kicked Nelly in the belly in the baaaarn,
'Cause the Old Man said it wouldn't do no
haaaarm . . .

"Say! Taday Grandpa goes back into retirement."

"Will you miss Broman's?"

"Yep. But it's silly fer two men ta work fer one
man's wages. Anyway, I gotta pull me some weeds
in the garden."

"I hope you make hash again." That wasn't
quite what I meant to say. I meant to tell him
I appreciated the good dinners he'd been making for us. But Grandpa wasn't used to compliments—giving or getting them—and I didn't
know how to say it.

The truck pitched and heaved up Broman's
rutted road. Grandpa's worn-out truck had no
shock absorbers, but he didn't seem to notice. He
was singing again.

"There's only one state in this great land of ours,
Where dreams can be realized.

The pioneers made it so for you and for me,
A legacy we'll always prize.
I'm singing, singing of you, singing of I-da-ho."

I didn't know why Grandpa was in such a good mood. Maybe he was proud that today I'd be on my own, and, like me about dinners, didn't quite know how to say so. Or maybe he was glad I'd be out of his hair.

Grandpa watched me harness the horses and hitch them to the wagon.

"Just wanted to make sure ya done it right." Grandpa limped off to the pickup. I felt a pang as I watched him back the truck, turn it sharp, and drive off. Working alone would be a lot different.

I eased the horses down the hill. My fingers were numb; I was holding the lines so tight the blood couldn't get through. Relax, I told myself, you don't want Mag and Tom to pick up your tension. I sang:

"I ain't got no mother,
    I ain't got no mother,
    I ain't got no mother
    To mend the clothes that I wear.

    I'm a poor lonesome cowboy,
    I'm a poor lonesome cowboy,

I'm a poor lonesome cowboy,
And a long way from home."

A mountain bluebird flew over, chirping.

"Now stand here, you guys, while I load the wagon," I ordered.

Tom and Mag stood in place for a moment, then Tom began to ease forward.

"Oh no, you don't. Back!" I hollered. I backed them to their original position. I tied the lines to the wagon bars and started loading again.

Tom sneaked ahead, pulling Maggie along. "Hey, cut that out!" I yelled. Tom had never questioned Grandpa's firmness, but he was testing me. I backed them into position again, but this time I didn't resume loading. I held the lines until Tom started to creep forward, then I gave the lines a sharp tug and ordered, "Whoa!" The horses stopped.

"We'll stand here until you decide not to move when I'm loading," I warned. I knew this was important, and I'd like to be able to tell Grandpa I'd handled it well. Grandpa didn't like bragging, so I'd have to recount it in a way that sounded modest.

After that I had no trouble. The horses stood quietly while I forked hay at each stop. They didn't attempt to go forward until I picked up my reins and gave them a signal. Grandpa said soon the horses would stop and go automatically— they'd know the feeding spots like an old-time milk horse knew its route.

When I was done feeding, I drove the wagon to the center of the field to practice. "Maggie," I called, and Maggie pulled off to the right. "Tom!" I yelled, and Tom, who was hooked on the left side, swung off left. Some men I'd watched at the fair used the words gee and haw— gee meant turn right, haw meant turn left. But Grandpa said that was for horses who didn't know their names.

The horses made tight turns around an old cottonwood. Then I drove them through a boggy area fed by an underground stream. Despite how much my balance had improved, I could barely keep my footing on the heaving wagon. Finally we came out on the side of a foothill. I took the horses up a narrow, overgrown path.

On the way down, the wagon ran up on Maggie. I jumped with fright, but Maggie remained calm, cautiously picking her way down the hill. She watched her step more closely than Tom; he often had his eye on distant places, as much as his blinkers allowed.

I needed to put the horses away. Not that I
planned to charge Broman for the time I'd spent
in training and practicing. But they'd worked
long enough.

I drove to the center again. It was easy to imag-
ine that huge lot as the state fair arena. The
crowd of flowering mule-ears on the hillsides
were thousands of spectators packed onto bleachers. The judge's stand would be in the middle
and in it, Miss Draft Horse, waiting to hand me
my trophy. When I leaned over to take it from
her she would whisper, "Your horses are so *beautiful!*"

Tom jumped and started to trot. Grandpa
would say, "Don't let 'im trot if ya ain't asked fer
a trot!" But I saw no harm in it—we were having
fun.

"Yay-hoo!" I hollered. The endless sky was
cloudless and, beyond the ranch, snowcapped
peaks jutted up to the sky.

Tom broke into a run. He pulled Maggie with
him.

"Hey," I yelled, "cut that *out!*"

They speeded up. I hauled on the lines as hard
as I could, but I was thrown down on my knees.
I tried to stand but couldn't; the wagon was going
too fast.

The worst thing you could have . . . Grandpa's

words came to me . . . was a runaway. I wondered if the horses would keep running, right through the fence we were charging up on. At nearly the last minute, Mag forced Tom to turn. Then the pair of them ran hell-bent alongside the fence.

A terrified lamb zigzagged in front of us. I heard a thud when the wheel struck it. Above the racket of the wagon I heard someone shouting—sounded like the word *mud*. Panic had shut down my mind and I couldn't think what that meant. Sheep, frightened by the clattering wagon, scattered everywhere. A wheel hit a rut and I flew off.

My head cracked on something hard, and I rolled over and over on a rocky field. When I came to rest, I heard moans and sobbing.

I looked up into the sun-baked face of Dusty Broman. That was when I realized the moans and sobs were my own.

"Don't move, son," he said. I tried to lift myself up onto my elbows. A white-hot pain seared my left side and I didn't cry anymore. Instead, I screamed.

CHAPTER 7

"It's a broke rib." Grandpa leaned over Broman's sofa, staring at me. Broman and his hired man, Manuel, had wrapped me in a blanket and carried me to the house and phoned Grandpa.

"You want us to take him up to Doc Richland's, Eldro?"

Grandpa shook his head. "There ain't nuthin' ta do fer a broke rib, noway. I'll wrap it up ta home. Dang fool kid! Did the horses git hurt?"

"The geldin' went down. But he didn't struggle, just lay there till Manuel got him up. He's scratched up and favorin' one leg, but I think he's just sore. The mare, she's okay."

"What happened?" Grandpa asked Broman. Besides the pain, I was feeling annoyed. The two men were talking like I wasn't there, or was dead or unconscious. Why didn't Grandpa ask *me* what had happened?

"The boy was doin' some practicin'. Next thing I knew, the horses took off. I yelled to head 'em into the mud—that would have slowed 'em down. But I guess he didn't hear me."

I coughed, and that made me moan in agony.

"Let's git 'im on home," Grandpa said.

Manuel and Broman put their arms under my shoulders and lifted me off the sofa. I had to bite my tongue to keep from crying out as they helped me to the truck.

Grandpa talked with Broman beside the barn for a few minutes, then he drove home as cautiously as possible. I could barely keep from gasping each time the truck found a rut.

Grandpa was dead silent. Why didn't he go ahead and say it? "That kid's nothin' but trouble. Ru-eent in one day all muh keerful trainin'."

Grandpa helped me into bed and went off to the kitchen to brew some coffee. Tears began to leak out of my eyes and run down my face. I couldn't keep from thinking about how we'd trained the horses, step by careful step. And how fast I'd undone it all.

When Grandpa delivered a cup to me a few minutes later, he stared at my face. I knew my eyes were wet and my nose was running.

"What's the matter, never saw anybody cry before?" I snapped.

"I s'pose I did. I'm lookin' at your eyeballs, ta
see if they're the same size. That's a purty good
lump on your head. Ya feel sick to your stomach?"

"Some. My eyeballs all right?"

"Yep. Did the fall knock ya out?"

"No."

He left then, and I slept awhile. But not long.
I woke up moaning. My side was killing me.

Grandpa brought me a bowl of soup and a
couple of aspirins. Over his shoulder he carried a
frayed old bandage.

"Ever'body on this road has wore this bandage.
Wellington's boy, your grandma, even Bess, muh
ole mare. You might's well, too. Sit up."

It hurt to sit up. But my upper belly did feel
some better after Grandpa wrapped it.

"Did I hit any lambs?"

"Three."

"Three? I thought one."

"Ya wasn't in no position ta count."

"Do we . . . do I have to pay for them?"

"Course! And Broman, he's a typical farmer.
He ain't agonna charge ya fer three puny lambs.
He's gonna charge fer what them lambs woulda
brung in the fall."

I moaned. Feeling stupid hurt almost as bad as
the rib. Not only had I messed up Maggie's and

Tom's training, I'd put myself deeper in debt.

"Am I fired?"

There was a knock on the door. Grandpa left, and a moment later I heard, "Well, Loretta, come on in! You, too, young feller!"

With the lump on my head, and scratches and bruises all over, I must have looked as bad as I felt. Because when Bobby Hodges's mother looked at me, her eyes filled with tears.

"Good gracious me, Andy!" she exclaimed, and bit her lip.

Behind her, Bobby put on a distressed-mother face. I chuckled, and pain shot up my left side.

"I know you probably don't feel up to eating," Mrs. Hodges said, "but Bobby and I brought you a plate of brownies. *Don't* get into those, Bobby. They're for Andy!"

I wanted them to leave so I wouldn't have to pretend it didn't hurt. But Bobby's mother pulled a chair up beside the bed and settled her plump backside into it.

"How's Dusty Broman?" she asked Grandpa. "I hardly see him around in the summer, he's so busy with his sheep. Here, Eldro, you have a brownie."

"Thankyuh, I will. Say, them're good. You remember Josie's chocolate cake, Loretta? She made the best chocolate cake in the valley."

"I remember it, Eldro. She brought that cake over when Mama was in the hospital."

"She used ta take that cake ever'where. To funerals, weddin's, the Fourth of July picnic. Got so folks 'ud hardly let her in anymore without that chocolate cake o' hers."

"When I was little, we kids thought Mrs. Pendrey was the nicest lady in the valley. There wasn't anybody didn't love her."

"Don't know how she ever took up with a ole cur like me." Grandpa looked out the window. When he wasn't scowling, he looked older, somehow. I think it was his eyes and the sorrowful look they took on. Grandma had died soon after I was born so I'd never known her. Grandpa only talked about her by accident. Then his sharp old features would soften up and he'd look like a forlorn pup.

Loretta Hodges smiled and patted Grandpa's hand. "We've got to go now, Eldro. Bobby'll be around tonight to check on Andy. You take care, you hear?"

"Am I fired?" I asked again after the Hodgeses left.

"Nope. But Broman ain't quite figgered out how ta git the feedin' done. He'll drive Maggie and Tom tamorry, but the day after he's gotta be gone. Manuel don't know how ta harness and drive, so I'll go over and help 'im. I'll drive, he'll fork hay. Day after that, they're both busy so . . ." Grandpa scowled. I could see he was wondering if he could load and feed hay by himself. The family honor was at stake. And he didn't want Broman to find someone to replace me—I still had to pay off those horses.

"I'll go," I said. I'd hoped to sound brave, but just then I had to cough. That twisted me up with pain, and I had to squeeze the bedpost and suck air until the stabbing quit. Then I tried again.

"I'll go," I said. "I can throw hay. My arm's not broken . . . just a rib." I tried to pull myself up straight and winced again. Breathing and the slightest movement sent bolts of pain tearing up my side.

Grandpa stared at me. He didn't mind staring in a way that probed your eyes, your face, maybe your guts. I got nervous as a gnat.

"Awright," he said finally. Just like that. No attempt to talk me out of it, no mention of my injury. "But not till day after tamorry." Then he left the room.

Nobody should make an offer he doesn't mean, especially to a man like Grandpa. It wasn't that I didn't mean it either. I just might have wished he

hadn't rushed into accepting it. I did want to get
back to working with Maggie and Tom. I did
want to make up for my mistakes, and I did want
to keep my bargain with Broman. But, aching
like I was with every breath, I just didn't know
how I could.

CHAPTER 8

Looking back, I don't know how I did it. Or why. I guess I was desperate to prove something.

Each time I breathed, stretched, or moved, gut-twisting pain ripped down my side. And since loading hay involved heavy breathing and constant stretching, every moment on the job was a torture. When I got home, I'd be so sore, even sitting quietly was a misery. After I went to bed, I woke up a lot, my side on fire.

The first day was the worst. I'd had two days of quiet at home and I dared to think my rib was much better. But just getting into the truck and riding to Broman's on the bumpy road showed me how wrong I was. I was shaking when we arrived.

The first time I reached up for a hay bale, the hurt was so bad sweat broke out on my face and tears filled my eyes. I thought I might not be able to reach for a second bale. I ground some enamel off my teeth and persuaded myself it wouldn't be as bad the second time. I grabbed a bale and threw it onto the wagon. A shooting pain doubled me over. I realized then that's how it would be—each bale would hurt more than the last.

Grandpa was watching me, hands in his pockets. I swallowed a tearful lump in my throat. Surely he could help, couldn't he? Maybe he figured it would hurt his old joints. More likely he thought there was a wonderful lesson in me doing it alone. For some reason, at that moment, I longed for my mom. She'd give me sympathy.

I couldn't think about completing the job. Instead I said to myself, That one hurt, but I'm still on my feet. I'll throw one more. Salty sweat poured into my eyes and my hands went numb from clenching my fists so hard. One more. And one more. And one more.

Then Grandpa lifted the reins. We were loaded. I sat down on the wagon's edge. Despite the bumps, the wagon felt like a rocking chair compared to the torture of loading hay.

Grandpa tried to find a smooth path to the feed yard. He watched me from the corner of his eye, but my head was too fuzzed with pain to figure out what his look said.

I felt twitchy inside. Whenever Grandpa

stopped the team and wrapped the lines on the wagon bar, I'd find myself scooting to the edge, ready to dive off if the horses started to go. That morning, when I'd stretched out my hand to pet Tom, I was surprised to see my fingers shaking. I was a town-raised kid who'd never even owned a pup, yet somehow I'd been able to trust big horses. I didn't anymore.

If Grandpa weren't stone silent all the time, I could ask him—when would the rib feel better? How long would I be scared from the accident?

I struggled through the morning and afternoon feeding and fell into bed that night, too miserable and sore to consider supper. Grandpa brought me a heaped-up plate of macaroni and cheese, but I waved it away. Then he handed me a letter from Mom. She'd gotten her grades from college, and she was proud of how she'd done. I read the pages in a haze of pain.

The ache in my side wouldn't let me sleep. I could hear in the kitchen the droning voices of Wellington Boyd and Grandpa. Wellington Boyd had started coming back in the evenings to drink coffee with Grandpa. He'd be moving soon, and his ties to Grandpa reached back so many years, he couldn't stay mad about the horses and face parting with Grandpa on bad terms.

I had tried to ease into a comfortable position

and was drifting off to sleep when I heard the screen door creak. I thought about raising myself on my elbow and trying to call Grandpa back. I suspected where he and Wellington were going. Every few months the valley's old-timers got together for a Saturday-night poker game. Whiskey and beer were part of the evenings. I knew Grandpa wouldn't be home until real late and tomorrow he'd have a hellacious hangover.

In the middle of the night I was startled awake when the front door swung open. Grandpa stumbled into the sofa, tripped over a cord, then bellowed like a bull. A moment later the light clicked on in my room. I pulled my blankets up protectively.

"HEY!" Grandpa stood over me, trying hard to focus on my face.

"Ya'll never guess what I done tonight!" His words were mushy.

"What?"

"I won! I won with four of a kind!"

He leaned close to me. I shrank from his potent breath.

"It's a omen. A *omen!*" He tapped my chest. "Means we're s'posed ta take them horses ta the state fair. Maggie 'n' Tom 'n' you 'n' me. *We're* four of a kind."

Did he mean it? Or was he just drunk?

"Used ta say me 'n' Josie was a pair o' aces. When your dad came along, we'd picked up another ace. *That* was a winnin' hand. Till Linden growed up ta where I couldn't understand 'im no more." Grandpa swayed above my bed like a pine in the wind.

"Then muh Josie up an' got cancer." He shook out his blue bandanna and honked his nose. "It's been solitaire ever since."

Grandpa rolled to the door, braced against the jamb, then stumbled to the sofa. When I got up to turn off my light, Grandpa was snoring—his cap and jacket still on.

I didn't even try to wake him Sunday morning—I knew it wouldn't do any good. I called Dusty Broman and told him Grandpa was sick and he wouldn't be able to get over to feed. He said, "I understand, Andy. I'd enjoy feedin' with the horses this mornin'. When Eldro's better later, you come on over and do the afternoon feedin'." It was plain he did understand.

Grandpa got up about three. He pulled himself to a sitting position and held his head in his hands for a long time. "Ya git anythin' ta eat?" he asked.

"Yeah."

"What about feedin'?"

"Dusty did it."

He steadied himself on the TV, shuffled out, and washed his face at the outside pump. He started for the truck and motioned for me to follow. We drove over to Broman's to do the afternoon feeding.

I doubted if he'd ever remember what he'd said about the horses when he was drunk. But when we were feeding he asked, "Reckon Maggie and Tom 'ud take ta the fair?"

"What about the runaway?"

"It's a setback, awright. But there's lots o' summer left ta work with. Four of a kind—that's quite a omen. 'Course we don't quite know about Tom yet, do we?"

I was so flattered I blushed. He'd hinted at something. That despite the accident, I was all right.

I didn't feel good long. When I thought it over, it seemed blind for Grandpa to think Tom was the unknown on our team. Looking at the record, who would take bets on a crippled old man, or on me?

CHAPTER 9

"Eighty percent o' horses won't do no good at a pullin' contest."

Grandpa gathered up the lines, clucked "Git up," and the horses moved off toward the feed-lot. Ever since Grandpa had admitted he wanted to take Maggie and Tom to the state fair's Draft Horse Pulling Contest, he'd talked a lot about our chances.

"A man kin have a good feed team er a plow team. He says ta hisself, 'I'll take this pair ta a pullin' contest.' Then, dollars ta doughnuts, they won't do no good."

"Why not?"

"They ain't keen on it."

"Percherons pull good, don't they?"

"Percherons is the smartest o' the draft horses. This nation was built on the backs o'

Percherons. But Shires has more fire to 'em.
Clydes pull good, and Belgians is strong and
doe-cile."

I moved to the back of the wagon bed to start
forking hay. The Grand Tetons loomed into view. The Tetons have their feet in Wyoming, but the best view of their peaks is from
Idaho.

"Sometimes horses just won't pull tagether,"
Grandpa went on. "A feller'll own a winnin'
horse. So he'll buy another winner ta go with it, ta
make a team 'at'll pull the lard outa pie crust. But
it don't seem ta work out. Them two great pullers
won't work tagether.

"Somethin' we might have agoin' fer us with
these two, if horse twins is like human twins, they
oughta be able ta communicate good."

Grandpa kept his eye on the horses. Ever since
the runaway, he watched them more closely than
he had even in their early training. I felt guilty
about the runaway all over again.

My rib didn't burn like before, but the steady
ache in my side wore me down so much I did
nothing but go to Broman's, then come home
and rest. Grandpa said he knew I was healing the
day I agreed to go fishing after work with Bobby
Hodges. Bobby and I caught a German brown

and four rainbows, but that wasn't the best part. The best part was I didn't notice my rib for about two hours.

Bobby asked me that morning, "You still interested in a job after you finish at Broman's? Squires are looking for a pipe mover."

"You bet," I said. "I've got a big debt on those horses, still." By the time Broman's sheep went on the forest, I would have earned $400, enough to pay off one horse. Except that Broman was deducting $200 from my wages to cover the cost of the lambs I'd hit. That meant I needed to earn $600 more.

Bobby and I stopped at Pat's General Store on the way home. Peggy Sundstrom collared me right away.

"Did those men find you yet?"

"What men?"

"Some forest rangers are looking for you."

"What'd I do?"

She shrugged. "I was the one told 'em where to find you."

"Thanks a lot."

Next day at Broman's, Grandpa and I were unhitching when a green car with black letters on the side drove up. Two uniformed men wearing badges got out. Grandpa, looking hostile, waited behind the horses.

"You Mr. Pendrey?" the older forest ranger asked. A young blond ranger reached around behind his boss and patted Maggie's rump.

"Ain't no use denyin' it."

"I'm Bob Reynolds, the forest supervisor. And this is Brant Jorgeson, a summer intern."

Grandpa looked at them blankly. Like all the valley's old-timers, he distrusted federal agencies and their men.

"Mr. Pendrey, we're looking around for a quiet pulling team, and isn't it fortunate we didn't have to look too far? The little girl at the general store told us you and your grandson have one. Let me explain why we're interested in them."

The young ranger opened his mouth, eager to speak, but the supervisor went on.

"We are planning some selective cutting in our forest district this year. A forest, as you know, is a complex ecosystem made up of many interdependent factors—soil, water, sunlight, insects, and trees. We are now beginning to appreciate how . . ."

Grandpa narrowed his eyes and squinted up at Reynolds. Then he turned his back on him, took the horses by their halters, and started to walk to the barn. I ran after him.

"Mighty interestin'," he muttered, "to find out forests is made up o' trees and bugs, but I'll have ta miss the rest."

"Mr. Pendrey!" the supervisor called. "Wait!"

Grandpa stopped and turned his head around slowly.

"Mr. Pendrey. Mother Nature has overplanted our forest in some places, resulting in overcrowding of trees. This is hard on grasses and bushes important to wildlife. We want to give nature a hand and allow healthier spacing of trees. We need to remove the overstoried growth so full sunlight can reach the forest floor."

Grandpa glowered at the forest supervisor. After a moment, Mr. Reynolds cleared his throat and went on.

"Machinery would disturb the natural soil balance and rip up other plant life. But the areas could be logged with horses with only minimum impact."

Grandpa shifted his gaze between the two men. Mr. Reynolds fingered the button on his shirtsleeve. The rangers waited expectantly for Grandpa to speak, but Grandpa could endure silence longer than they could.

I was interested, so I spoke up.

"You want to hire Grandpa and me to do some logging up on the forest?"

"That's it exactly."

Grandpa started to speak, but I cut him off. "How much does it pay?"

"You'd have to sell the wood yourself," Mr. Reynolds answered. "But I know of a man looking to buy wood and willing to pick it up on the mountain, so you wouldn't have to worry about trucking it out. You'd probably skid several hundred dollars' worth of trees per week."

My head started to calculate—enough to pay off the horses, enough to . . . Grandpa's washboard voice broke into my figuring.

"Nope. Too dangerous." With that, he turned and walked the horses to the barn.

Brant, the young ranger, spoke up.

"Logging with horses is dangerous, but your grandpa looks like . . ."

". . . like nothing would scare him."

"Yeah."

"I don't know why he said no so quick. Let me go talk to him. Don't go away."

Grandpa didn't look up from brushing Tom.

"Grandpa, that would be enough money to pay off the horses and buy hay for winter or make a down payment on Boyd's wagon."

"Maybe. But we can't go live in the woods the rest of the summer."

"Why not?"

"We got ourselves a fence ta build, fer one thing."

"We could do that in the fall. We could finish a small corral now, then make it bigger later."

"I got a garden ta tend. That's Josie's patch and I've kept it planted ever' summer since she died. And summer's when muh arthritis don't hurt and I kin git out to the cemetery ever' day ta visit Josie's grave."

Normally I swallowed down words that might get me in trouble. But this time, I spoke up.

"I'd like to go by myself, Grandpa."

Grandpa's spidery hand gripped the curry brush hard. "That right?"

"Because ever since the runaway I"—I wound a strap around my palm—"I've been, um, scared of Maggie and Tom. And if I worked with them every day, by myself, I'd get over it. Otherwise . . ." I scraped my throat, "it will end up they're your horses. And I want them to be my horses."

Without looking at me, Grandpa handed me a harness to hang up.

"Yup," he said, and his voice quavered. He motioned for me to follow him. When he spotted the rangers, he squared his shoulders, but his leg dragged and something in the droop of his arm looked sorrowful.

Mr. Reynolds came forward. "Mr. Pendrey, if you'd like to ride up and see the . . ."

"I would," Grandpa said, and limped over to the government car.

At forest headquarters, we got into a four-wheel-drive vehicle. The truck rolled up a narrow fire lane and my side started to throb. Grandpa gazed out the window in silence. Mr. Reynolds talked, trying to sell Grandpa on the logging idea.

"What equipment would we need, Grandpa?"

"Nothin' we ain't got. A chain saw, a log chain, a grabhook."

The blond ranger turned off the engine. "Here's our place." He pointed to a timbered cliffside.

Grandpa bent back his head and gazed up the hill.

"I hope this is the worst place ya plan ta log."

"Actually, it's the best of the three," Brant grinned.

"Be tricky to lay out skid trails here."

"I'd be happy to help with the planning. Last semester I did a lot of reading on it, and it will be my job to approve the trails."

Grandpa turned to me. "I'd have ta teach ya a awful lot before ya come up here."

Mr. Reynolds looked startled.

"Mr. Pendrey, you don't mean you're thinking of sending the boy up here by himself?"

"I'm thinkin' about it."

"Well, I'm certain an arrangement like that simply wouldn't work for us. We have a responsibility to make sure it's a safe operation. There's a liability issue, you know. We'd have to be dealing with an adult. We can't assume risks to children."

"If I sign the contract, I kin hire whoever I want, can't I? Then the risk is mine."

"That's a risk you're willing to assume?"

"I'd help look out for Andy," Brant put in.

Mr. Reynolds frowned. "Mr. Pendrey, I won't pretend we wouldn't like to contract with you and your team. It would take us weeks or months to try to find someone else. But I'm a father, too, and I can tell you that logging in these conditions is nothing I'd consider allowing my son to do."

"I ain't askin' ya to. I kin tell *you*, the first time I skidded logs with a team, I was eight years old, not near as big er as smart as Andy says he is."

On the way back to Broman's, Grandpa and Mr. Reynolds worked out the details of the contract. Work would begin the week Broman's sheep went on the forest. I would provide my own food and a place to stay (I'd take Grandpa's tepee). Brant would take me to town once a week

to get supplies and see Grandpa. Grandpa tried
to persuade them to give me a weekly salary so
I'd be guaranteed a wage, but Mr. Reynolds held
firm. He said how much money I made would
depend on how hard I worked.

We were doing the dishes that night when
Grandpa said, "Five more days at Broman's. Ya
think ya'll miss it?"

"Yeah, I will."

"Me, too. How's the rib?"

"Better every day."

"I wasn't quite ready ta have ya go off on your
own."

I slowed down wiping a plate.

"I don't mean it ain't a good thing fer a boy."
He handed me a dripping cup. "I just hope it's
the right thing."

CHAPTER 10

Grandpa said he was showing me how to skid logs with my horses. It seemed he was trying to scare me to death.

"Loggin' might be the easiest way in the world ta git killed," he told me. "Ya got ta be awatchin' ever' minute, ever' minute.

"Never be downhill from the log you're draggin'. Never walk off ta one side—the log kin swing around an' hit ya an' break a leg. Be careful with this here grabhook—don't git your leg with it instead o' the log.

"But the biggest hazard ya need ta watch out fer is trees. One comes down on ya, don't expect ta live through it."

"Brant said I'll be wearing a hard hat at all times."

"Holy Moses! Ya think that'd do a bit o' good if a tree fell on ya?"

"I'll cut them how you said, so they'll fall away from me."

"Land Awmighty! Must be nice ta be twelve years old and know ever'thin'! Shut up about a minute and I'll tell ya how ta keep your head on your neck.

"A green tree—it's purty purdictable." With a stick, he drew in the dust. "Ya put a notch in 'er here, and a notch in 'er here on the opposite side. When she starts ta topple, the hinge in the middle o' the tree'll make 'er go this way." He motioned left. "Er this." Right. "It can't go like this er this." He flung his hand backward and forward.

"But a dead tree can be squirrelly. That hinge in the middle might bust clean away, so the tree kin come down any which aways."

"So you always have to stand far off?"

"Ya stand up *close,* so if the tree does somethin' ya don't expect, ya take one and a half steps around and you're safe. Ya couldn't outrun it if you was in its path.

"Another thing ya oughta know about is 'widow makers.' Sometimes when a tree topples, it'll land against another tree, strip off a branch, and send the branch flyin' like a bullet."

"When you were logging, anybody on your crew ever get hurt?"

"I helped bring down ole Henry Cassidy. He was loggin' up on Pine Mountain when a 'widow maker' got 'im. He didn't suffer none—it killed 'im right off."

I didn't have anything to say for a while. Finally I asked, "Well, is logging any fun at all?"

"Fun! Ya won't think ya never worked hard in your life till ya skid logs. Only way ta make money is ta keep movin'. Start early and walk all day, up and down the mountain."

"So, I need to watch out for dead trees and widow makers. Anything else?"

"Yeah. Ya need to know about the wind. The wind can change a safe siteation inta a deadly one."

On my last day feeding sheep, Dusty Broman came up when I was unharnessing and petted Maggie and Tom.

"This is a fine team, Andy. The mare, I think, could pull with the best of them. And this geldin' has surprised me."

Tom had become heavier, and he'd lost his dark hair. A dapple gray coat had grown in. The grain mixture Grandpa fed, plus rich grazing, had put a gleaming coat on both horses.

Broman shook Grandpa's hand, handed me my last check, and gripped my shoulder.

"You've been a trooper, Andy. I'd be pleased to have you back next year." He looked at Grandpa questioningly. Grandpa only shrugged.

Why didn't Grandpa say sure we'd be back? Didn't he want me in Dove Valley next summer?

Brant Jorgeson dropped by the cabin that evening to see how things were going. Brant would do the inspections on my logging, and he was excited to get on with it. But I worried a little about his reaction when I told him the safety warnings Grandpa had given me.

"Of course you have to take reasonable safety precautions. But as to some of your grandpa's ideas, they're out-of-date. We have scientific knowledge now that takes a lot of the guesswork out of logging."

"You mean you can pretty well tell what trees are going to do?"

He smiled. "That's what I go to school for."

Brant offered a Forest Service horse trailer to haul Maggie and Tom to the mountains. He said it was a large trailer, but when Maggie and Tom were loaded into it, it looked cramped.

We threw my gear into the pickup's bed. Then Grandpa motioned me to follow him over behind the aspens, out of earshot.

His face was so solemn and his eyes so worried, I thought he was going to ask me if I'd made a will, or had any last words to say before I disappeared onto the mountain. But what he did was give me parting advice about the horses.

"Andy, I'm gonna tell ya somethin' now that Roy Chatlosh told me once. And I've awwus tried ta live by it." Roy Chatlosh was an old man in his mid-eighties who usually won at state fair pulling contests. He was known around Idaho as the man who'd forgotten more about draft horses than most folks had ever known. He was a jolly, elfish man, and everybody called him Uncle Chatty.

Grandpa's brows linked above his nose and his eyes bored into mine.

"Here's what he told me. He said, 'Eldro, ya kin sometimes lie ta your friends, though it ain't a good idee. And ya kin lie ta your wife, but not too much. But don't never, *never* lie ta your horses!' "

My face must have told him I didn't have the least idea what he meant.

"Andy, them horses trust ya. They'll do what ya ask of 'em. So don't never ru-een their confidence by tellin' 'em ta do somethin' they can't. The best way ta ru-een horses' confidence is ta git 'em stuck. The work on the forest'll be good fer 'em, git 'em in shape fer the state fair. As long as ya don't lie to 'em."

I promised I wouldn't lie to Maggie and Tom.

*   *   *

Brant and I agreed to eat dinner together that night and share the cooking and cleanup. I'll admit I was surprised to see how much help a man seven years older than me needed. There was the coffee thing, for instance.

"I sure would feel more at home if I had a cup of coffee," Brant said.

"Did you forget to bring coffee?" I asked.

"No. But I forgot the coffeepot."

"Well," I said, "you could empty the coffee grounds into a sack, then use the can to boil water. Dump in some grounds and you've got coffee."

"What does it taste like?"

"Grandpa's coffee. Um, you been in the mountains much?"

"No, this is my first summer. I was raised in Chicago, but I've always loved the mountains and dreamed of doing this. We'll have a great time!"

Brant was staying in a Forest Service cabin about three miles away. He suggested I leave the horses tied and come share his cabin, but of course I couldn't do that. Maggie's nostrils were aquiver with the tingling mountain air and a thousand new scents, and even the normally placid Tom was blowing and stomping. If they got scared in the night, they could break their halters and run away.

Grandpa had shown me how to set up his canvas tepee. I found some tall aspen logs to use as poles, trimmed them with my ax, and lifted the tepee. Brant looked impressed.

"Little Brave very clever," he said.

After supper and dishes, Brant dragged a log up beside the fire, reached into his jacket, and pulled out something. He put it to his lips and a thin, melancholy sound flowed out.

"What's that?" I asked.

"A tin whistle. Now, Maestro Jorgeson will play, for your edification, a concert of all-time favorite melodies. After which, I will pass the hat for donations. To help with my tuition." I laughed.

He played "Sweet Molly Malone," "Home on the Range," "America the Beautiful," "Amazing Grace," and more. The notes floated into the campfire and rose with the smoke to linger in the crowns of trees. My stomach was quiet—I had a feeling of belonging here.

Finally Brant got up, waved good-bye, and walked off to his pickup without taking the whistle from his lips. It sounded like a night bird flying past.

I fed Maggie and Tom their grain, and for the

first time understood what Grandpa meant when
he talked about horses being dependent on their
owners. When a coyote howled on a peak above
us, the horses crowded close to me. Lodgepoles
swayed and creaked around us.

"It's all right, Mag," I said, rubbing her head.
"It's all right, Tom."

I crawled into my sleeping bag and lay watching
a fistful of stars shining through where the poles
stretched the canvas. It felt strange to be all alone.
During dinner Brant had told me about a sheep-
herder who had his tent slashed by a bear the previous summer. I knew Maggie and Tom would
smell a bear or any other wild animal and alert me.
But it did feel odd and scary to be so far from anyone else. I hoped my appendix wouldn't bust, or
something like that, because I wouldn't be able to
get help and I'd die right there on the mountain.

Sometime in the night I woke up. Wind was
battering the tepee. I heard a boom of thunder
and a horse's scream. I started to crawl out of the
tepee, then remembered I should take a coat or a
rain slicker and spent a few minutes pawing
through my pack searching for one. I settled for
a heavy woolen shirt Grandpa had sent along.

The horses were prancing back and forth on
their tether line, stretching it to the breaking
point, and neighing frantically. The farthest

they'd ever been from home was the five miles to
Broman's, and in this new place the wild wind
and smell of the storm put them in a lather.

I pulled on their ropes and brought them close.
"Easy," I whispered, "I won't let the storm hurt
you." I wished I believed my words. Lightning
crashed above the gaunt trees, making me
cringe—if a bolt struck one of them, the three of
us would be fried.

I was relieved when the lightning passed and
the rain started. But cold pelting rain didn't ease
the horses' fear. Rain beat against my back, but I
didn't think I could leave Maggie and Tom.

I hoped the storm would last only a few minutes, but it was a full-fledged cloudburst. Icy
streams ran down my back and soaked my T-
shirt. My jeans, saturated with water, pressed
heavy against my legs. I began to shake with
cold. My fingers, buried in the horses' drenched
necks, grew numb. I couldn't murmur sooth-
ing words—my teeth were chattering too hard.
But I stayed.

After the storm passed, I stripped off my
clothes, jumped into the tepee, and huddled in
my sleeping bag. I was too drowsy to wiggle, but
I did have one sleepy thought as I drifted off.
Tomorrow was my first day on a new job, and
again I'd be dog-tired.

CHAPTER 11

Gargling sandhill cranes woke me at dawn, despite my interrupted night's sleep. At our cabin in Dove Valley, it was so quiet in the mornings I could have slept till noon every day if Grandpa would have let me. But in the forest, the creaking trees, rumbling stream, and bawl of far-off cattle made a racket I couldn't shut out. I reread my latest letter from Mom. She was hoping she could send me a bus ticket so I could visit her in Ohio. I pulled dry clothes from my pack and dressed.

I crept out of my tepee, carrying soaked boots. I had no choice, I had to wear them cold and soggy.

"Hi," I yawned to Maggie and Tom. They nickered an answer. I broke the skin of ice on their water tub and added more water. Maggie drank well; Tom only sniffed it.

"You got a real day ahead of you, Tom," I

warned. "You can have all you want now, but Grandpa says you only get sips later, so drink up." Tom lifted the tub with his teeth and its contents sloshed over my already saturated boot.

"Quit it, dummy!" I pretended to threaten Tom with my fist. The memory of the runaway haunted me still, but Maggie and Tom had trusted me during the storm. Maybe I could learn to rely on them, too.

I fed them, then gathered wood for a fire. Mosquitoes buzzed around my ears, face, and hands. Once my fire was blazing, I escaped into its smoke to fix breakfast. I ate three eggs, a half-package of sausage, and some bread. Then I cooked up the same amount again. Either I'd have to curb my appetite or I'd run out of supplies before the end of the week.

The sun bounced up over a peak just as I finished eating. I put on my jacket and walked over to the first slope I'd be logging. I did what Grandpa had told me—studied where the weight was on the trees, searched their crowns for booby traps, and tried to decide where my first skid trail would be. I chose four trees to practice on.

Once I'd decided where to notch them, the cutting was simple and fast. The trees weren't very wide, so the chain saw buzzed through them like a knife in warm butter. I didn't cut them all the way—Grandpa said it gave him the willies to see weekend woodcutters do that. There was a difference between felling trees and merely cutting them down, he said. I was proud when the first trees I'd ever cut fell just where I'd planned they would, with their butt ends together and accessible to chain up and drag off.

I was scared to try my hand at hauling logs, but I couldn't put it off any longer. I went back and began harnessing Maggie and Tom. Then I had a change of heart and sat down on a rock. I scolded myself for the fear I felt about working the horses alone. I went back to harnessing. But I moved real slow.

The sun was warming the mountainside when I heard a bird warbling in the pines behind me. The call became louder with more notes to it. Suddenly, it turned into "Yankee Doodle." Brant stepped out of the trees, laughing and waving his tin whistle.

"Morning, Andy!"

He ran his fingers over Maggie's harness. He piped the first few measures of "The Old Gray Mare."

"Hey, tell me what all this stuff is."

Starting at Maggie's head, I explained.

"These are the blinds, this in her mouth is a bit, the reins here, the hame, the collar, the back pad, the bellyband, the back strap, hip straps, then the tugs, the pinery hook, and heel chain."

"You know how to put this contraption on all by yourself? Could I try it someday, just so I could say I did it once?"

"Sure."

I pointed to the slope. "I went ahead and cut some green trees near the top."

"Come on. Let's go check your stumps," Brant said.

I walked behind as he inspected.

"Hmmm, about twelve inches high—looks good. Why'd you cut these at such a sharp angle?"

"Because I want the logs I'm dragging to roll over them."

Brant nodded. "Clever. Carry on."

I wanted to keep looking good in Brant's eyes, but as soon as I began to skid logs, I showed what a first-class beginner I was. Nothing worked like it had at home. My fingers fumbled as I hooked three logs up to the chain, and I had to repeat the procedure several times before the logs were hooked together right. Then, when I took my place behind Maggie and Tom, my hands on the reins were shaky. I clucked for them to git up. The logs didn't pull into a neat bundle like Grandpa had showed me, but spraddled out over the rocks and stumps. Maggie sidestepped in fright. I looked around for an excuse to put the horses away. The sky was cloudless, and Brant was watching me expectantly.

In those first hours Tom stopped often, laid his ears back, and turned around to give me a dirty look. I felt nervous then, wondering if Tom might test me again. I knew I must be confusing him with my commands because I was so confused myself.

Brant sat on a rock, calling suggestions now and then. I was so mad at how things were going, I pretended not to hear him. Once he jumped down to give me a hand when a log hung up on a rock. "I'll get it!" he yelled and ran over to free the log. Just then the horses pulled it loose and it swung in an arc and struck him in the thigh.

"Ouch!" he hollered, and jumped away. He was lucky, it only bruised him. But I was relieved when he got in his pickup and left.

By noon I had only made two trips down the slope. The way I was working, I would have made more money staying home and moving irrigation pipe.

We were moving up the slope when all of a sudden Maggie jumped sideways. A limb in the path had snapped up and stabbed her in the belly. I ran to see if she was hurt. A long scratch on her underside was bleeding slightly. Grandpa had told me to keep my path free of limbs, but my head was so busy trying to remember a hundred other things, I forgot about that. I decided to put Mag and Tom up for a while.

I opened a can of beans for lunch and spooned them into my mouth, wondering what I was doing in such a forsaken place and why I'd thought I'd be able to do the job myself. If I messed up with Maggie and Tom again, I'd ruin the team for good.

Sitting there swatting at yellow jackets, I convinced myself the whole mess was Grandpa's fault. He knew how rough logging was—he should have told me I couldn't come up by myself. Or how about Dad? I was supposed to be in his care, and he didn't even know where I was.

The afternoon went better, but only a little. I still moved up and down the hill at a turtle's pace. Maggie and Tom were fresh as they'd been that morning. It'd take a lot better man than me to tire them.

Late afternoon, something happened that shook me. I'd just sawed a forty-foot dead lodgepole when a gust of wind came up. I was watching the tree's crown, as Grandpa stressed I should, when the gust caught the tree midair, spun it, and sent it flying opposite from where I'd planned it would fall. I was able to step to the other side of the trunk and get out of its path, but the episode destroyed the confidence I'd picked up about being able to fell trees where I wanted them to go.

I was too edgy that night to make a cook fire. I sat on a log cramming chocolate chip cookies into my mouth and wondering. What was Grandpa doing? Worrying? About me, or only Maggie and Tom?

Last night's storm had convinced me I needed to rig up a shelter for the horses, like Grandpa said. I hung a tarpaulin between two trees. With my handsaw, I cut up dead branches to nail together for a manger. I was tying the manger into place when I heard a birdlike trill in the trees. I cocked my head and listened. I turned toward the clearing, expecting Brant's grinning, sunburned face to appear in the moonlight.

After a few minutes, I realized the song had come from a real bird, not Brant's whistle. Being around Grandpa had turned me superstitious about warnings and omens. A bird singing in the dark struck me as eerie. I went to bed feeling jumpy and alone.

CHAPTER 12

It took every ounce of my time and energy during those first couple of weeks to learn what I was supposed to be doing. When I was felling trees or driving the team, I had to concentrate so hard my brain felt like it would bust. When I crawled into my sleeping bag at night, problems from the day swirled in my head. I guess I ate, drank, and slept logging.

On Saturdays, when Brant drove me to town for supplies and a visit with Grandpa, Grandpa would ask if the horses were in good flesh, how many logs I was bringing down, and what I might have earned that week. Hearing me tell about a limb that fell out of a sixty-foot-tall tree and almost hit me or about Maggie throwing a shoe and me searching for it an entire afternoon, reminded Grandpa of some fresh tale from his logging days.

I liked the look on Brant's face when Grandpa was telling a yarn. Brant would scooch in close to Grandpa's metal table, suck the rim of his coffee cup, and bob his head.

"That was a great story!" he'd say on our trip back to the timber. "He's really authentic, isn't he? I mean, he was there, on the frontier, and those people had guts."

I had Brant to thank for the few carefree times I had. He forced me to go fishing with him and insisted I go along on his nature walks. He showed up for these walks with an armload of books.

"What's all this?" I'd ask.

"*Birds of the Rockies, Wildflowers of the Rockies, Rocks of the Rockies,* trees, brush, insects. Look at this bird book. See? A color illustration of a Clark's nuthatch. All the books have pictures like that. You're going to help me get some good out of them. They cost me a fortune."

I was too tired after work to try and identify butterflies, but I liked trailing after Brant and looking at the pictures he found. At first he had a hard time spotting anything, but in only a week he got better. He couldn't do like Grandpa— Grandpa could say, "Is there an eagle circlin' up there behind me?" without even turning around. But Brant got so he'd whisper "Freeze!" in the middle of a conversation and I'd have to be stone-still until he located in the book some bird or insect he'd spied.

With so much to occupy my mind, I might have forgotten about the pulling contest if it hadn't been for Maggie and Tom. Working with them every day, watching how strong and capable they had become, I couldn't help but remember my dreams of taking them to the state fair. The dream whispered to me: *They're in great shape. Look how tough they've become. Nobody will say they're only puny twins.*

"Can't we get dinner going?" Brant asked me one night when I was giving the horses a saltwater rubdown on their shoulders.

"Nope. Grandpa says I have to take care of the horses first."

Brant shrugged and squeezed out a rag for me.

"Will you be able to get all this timber down before you go back to school?"

"Some of it will probably have to wait for next year. I want to quit up here in time to get ready for the fair." I hadn't meant to confide my fair plans, but after I'd blurted that out, Brant pressed me with so many questions I finally told him all about the pulling contest.

"How many people come and watch?" he asked.

"The bleachers are packed. It's the biggest event at the fair."

"How much money could you win?"

"Three hundred and fifty dollars for first, three hundred for second, two-fifty for third, two hundred for fourth." The money was only a part of it, but I didn't say that. More important was that winning would make me somebody.

"Do you have a pretty good chance?"

"I think Maggie and Tom can do it. Grandpa does, too. But the competition is tough."

"Wow! I might come and watch. I'd be back in school, but maybe I could come down for that one day. Labor Day, you say. Let's see—I could drive all night . . ."

His interest encouraged me to tell fair stories while we were eating.

"There's an old man in his eighties—everybody calls him Uncle Chatty. He's set some pulling records. And it's funny about him—most guys yell at their horses to urge them on. But Uncle Chatty just goes like this . . . *smoooch*. He says you have to treat your horses like you would a girl— just give 'em a sweet kiss—*smooooch*—like that, and they'll do anything to please you."

Brant threw back his blond head and laughed.

"Whoo, I've *got* to come see this. It's not every day a guy gets to watch a friend and two horses he's lived with all summer compete in something like that."

Suddenly I was embarrassed. I was Brant's friend, not just a nuisance kid. I cleared my throat, but when I spoke, my voice squeaked anyway. "It'd be real nice to have you come."

When Brant returned next morning, he looked solemn and tired. In the three weeks I'd been on the forest with him, he'd never yet been without a cheery greeting for me. But he trudged up to my camp piping a gloomy march on his whistle.

"Hi." I finished snapping buckles on my harness. "You all right?"

"Yeah. Fine." He stared up at fleecy clouds pushing through the wide blue sky. "It feels kinda funny out today, you notice?"

I hadn't. But I moved over to Maggie and Tom protectively, and rechecked their buckles, bridles, and bitting. I gazed skyward to where Brant was staring, and a shiver zipped across my back. It was the way Brant's blond head was profiled against the sky.

I was glad I'd brought my jacket along, because about ten o'clock a chilly wind began to moan in the trees. I never cut trees if the wind was strong, but these were infrequent gusts. I started trying to fell as many as I could in case a storm kicked up later in the afternoon.

Brant came around to check my stumps. He absently recorded numbers on his government sheet.

"Are you all right?" I asked again.

He shrugged. "Andy, do you think we'll ever have another summer like this one?"

"All summers are good, 'cause you don't have to go to school."

He almost smiled. "But what if I don't find a job like this, after I graduate, and I have to go back and live in the city?"

"You'll find a job out here."

He nodded. Then he walked over to a boulder. He laid his papers down and began to make more notes.

"That's too close to where I'm cutting," I hollered.

"But you're felling trees that way," he pointed.

The wind whined in the trees above me. "This wind makes me jumpy. Would you clear out of the area until I'm done?"

He walked back over to my side and for the first time that morning, grinned.

"You always forget. I'm here to keep my eye on

you. You're out of line, Private, giving me orders. Now, carry on."

About a half hour later I saw the top of Brant's yellow hard hat moving toward me. Brant was walking head down, his eyes buried in paperwork. I only glanced at the yellow hat—I was watching the wavering crown of a tree I'd just cut. The tree was starting to fall with its butt end to the trail, like I'd planned—until a strange train-engine noise wailed in the trees above me. Then the wind grabbed the falling tree, spun it around, and sent it toppling in the opposite direction.

"BRANT!" I screamed. *"LOOK OUT!"* For a long second the yellow hat continued to bob toward me. Then my warning registered with Brant and he lifted his chin. His eyes searched the treetops. His face contorted in a soundless scream.

"Here!" I yelled, but Brant had started to run back toward the boulder. I remembered to step to the opposite side of the tree only a second before a tornado sound thundered in my ears. The tree slammed to earth beside me.

The falling tree had kicked up so much dust and leaves I couldn't see. I'd heard no scream. I'd heard a yip, like a coyote's but couldn't tell if it had been in the distance or had come from Brant.

"Brant?" I called, and began to walk the length of the tree. A moment later my stomach lurched. Lying amid pinecones and scrub plants was a pair of booted feet.

"Mom," I moaned. "Dad. Grandpa." I thought I'd be sick, but I forced down the sourness in my chest and moved over to check my friend.

He was pinned under the tree. He was lying faceup, his arms splayed, his face bluish. The tin whistle was smashed beside him.

"Brant!"

His eyelids fluttered, then he turned his head slightly.

"Andy," he gasped, and it seemed to take all his air to say the word. His mouth was open and he was panting.

"Don't let me die . . . Andy," Brant whispered.

I needed to get the tree off him fast. I walked the length of it. When I reached its end, I stopped dead. The top was wedged into a cleft between two boulders.

I considered: Could I fit a saw blade in between the boulders to saw off the tree's crown? Or use a handsaw to take off the limbs, then lift the trunk out?

"Don't worry, Brant, we'll get you out. I'll be right back." As I walked to where the horses were

tied, I ticked off methods that wouldn't work. It
was too narrow between the boulders for sawing.
Sawing farther down, by Brant, was too dangerous. Even as I planned what I would do, I was
denying I'd have to. Worms coiled around my
guts. Yet, aware of how alone I was and who
depended on me, I untied the horses and headed
them up to where Brant lay.

I'd have to move the boulder. I had no idea
what a boulder would weigh—I only knew
Grandpa and I had once tried to move a rock for
fun—a rock a fourth the size of those boulders,
and Grandpa had quit after a minute because he
was afraid we'd stick the horses.

As I drove Maggie and Tom up the hill, I didn't
fill their heads with pleas and promises. I was
dead silent, feeling grimmer than I knew possible. The horses picked up my mood. Tom usually waggled his ears with curiosity when I got
behind him and he knew he was going to work.
But that day he only thumped up the hill like a
horse going to battle. Maggie's rump tensed—the
lines connecting me to her carried a message of
desperation.

Brant was saying something. I couldn't take
the time out to go listen, but I caught a few
words—"questions . . . hard . . . big test."

I maneuvered Maggie and Tom into position.

I dropped the lines and the horses stood motionless while I wrapped the chain around the boulder. When I picked up the lines, a dark thought swept my mind. I'd never be able to move the rock. Brant would die. That idea made me shake so much my knees almost folded under me. I tried to cluck to my team, but no sound came out of my trembling lips. Yet, Tom perked his ears and then lowered his head. Maggie turned her head slightly toward Tom, as though he had spoken to her.

I thought, If ever in your life you'll need to pull—it's now. If you do this for me, I'll never again ask another hard thing from you.

They were small for their age, and young. Grandpa had said, "Don't ever lie to 'em," but this was different. I squeezed my eyes shut.

When I opened them, Maggie was trying to crawl across the hill like an earthworm. Tom was lathered from his neck to his tail with sudsy foam. I didn't know how long I should let them try. I suspected that for me they'd keep trying until their lungs busted.

Finally I found my voice. It was only a whisper.

"Dear God, *please*," I pleaded. I saw both their rumps constrict and the already knotted muscles in their shoulders pop and bulge. Through my tears, I saw the stone begin to move.

"*Go!*" I yelled.

They pulled it far enough. I ran to them and slackened the chain. The boulder teetered and started to slip. After a moment it rolled, then crashed down the hillside, pulverizing trees in its path.

I ran to the tree pinning Brant and tried to lift it. I couldn't. What now? I dashed over, grabbed the lines, and backed the horses. If I dragged the tree off Brant, couldn't that make his injuries worse? I attached the chain to the log, then ran it across the remaining boulder.

"Pull!" I ordered, and Maggie and Tom lifted the tree cleanly into the air like it was a toothpick.

I heard Brant moan. When I looked at him now, my blood turned to ice. He was purple and gasping for breath. I knelt beside him and placed my hand on his chest. My fingers came back soaked with blood.

"Brant."

"Don't . . . let . . . me . . . die," he rasped. Then he moaned something about being late for class.

There were so many things to do—find out what was wrong with his breathing and where the blood was coming from. And how would I get him down the mountain?

Next moment I was zigzagging through the trees, leaping over bushes. I prayed Brant's truck would hold a first aid kit, as well as the radio I could use. I flung open the truck door. Brant's keys were in the ignition. I started the engine, lifted the receiver, and flicked the switch.

"Help." It was a whimper. I forced air into my lungs.

"*Help!* This is Andy Pendrey and I need help for Brant. Fast. A tree fell on him."

Only static answered me. I stared at the radio. Maybe it wasn't tuned to the right channel. It had a hundred buttons. I was reaching out to punch one when a woman's voice asked, "Where are you, Andy?"

"Three miles north from the guard station and a mile east of Wolf Creek."

"Can we land a rescue copter?"

"There's a clearing where I've been logging."

"What are Brant's injuries?"

"He's bleeding and can't breathe good."

"Mr. Reynolds is on his way. Try to stop the bleeding with pressure. Are you all right?"

I threw down the receiver and turned off the engine. I found a first aid kit under the seat and raced back to Brant.

I drew out a pocketknife and slit Brant's shirt. Brant moaned. His chest was soaked in blood. I couldn't tell where it was coming from.

"Hang on, Brant. Help's coming."

"Paper . . . due, today," Brant gasped.

It seemed like hours before I heard a truck's engine at the bottom of the hill. Then, someone running. Mr. Reynolds pulled me off Brant, a little roughly.

Suddenly cold, I huddled next to the boulder and shivered. It seemed I was watching Mr. Reynolds through a curtain.

"Turn paper . . . in . . . for me," Brant choked.

"Don't worry, Brant, I will," Mr. Reynolds promised. He leaned close to Brant's face and frowned. "How long has he been out of his head?"

"Off and on awhile." He probably thought it was my fault. He never wanted to hire a kid in the first place.

"Respiration seriously compromised," Reynolds mumbled. "Probably a punctured lung. If help doesn't get here soon . . ." He rolled up a blanket, pressed it against Brant's chest, and tied it in place with a bandage. Brant's color had worsened and his breathing sounded like gargling.

Reynolds wrapped a blanket around my shoulders. "Your grandpa's coming up. I sent Morrison after him."

It seemed I sat there for hours, listening to

Brant fight for air. The forest held its breath. No
birds chattered, the wind didn't stir, the stream
had shut itself off.

Then came the whir of the copter. Two para-
medics in blue jackets jumped from it before it
was completely stopped. They knelt over Brant,
checked this and that, and in only moments were
back to the copter carrying Brant on a stretcher.
The helicopter lifted off, disappeared above the
pines, and all was still again.

Mr. Reynolds sat on a dead log, jabbing at ants
with his toe.

"Will . . . Brant make it?"

He took a long time to answer. His jawbones
stuck out from his face and his eyes were wet.
"That copter will have . . . to be fast. If they can
get him to a hospital, maybe . . ."

"If he lives, will he be . . . all right?"

He gave me a warning scowl.

We sat in silence until Grandpa arrived. The
old man limped over to me. He squinted at me
hard.

"All right?" he asked.

I nodded.

He swiveled his head around, looking over the
accident scene. He hobbled to the fallen tree's
stump and studied it. He peered up at all the
remaining trees. Then he walked the felled tree's

length. He came to the hole where the boulder had been.

For several minutes he stared at the hole, his lips moving. I'd said the boulder was four times bigger than the one Grandpa and I had tried to move at home. But when I'd seen the hole it left, I knew I'd been wrong. That rock had been ten times as big. When we began to pull it, I'd had no idea how much of it was buried. Now Grandpa, peering into that hole, was putting together the story of Brant's entrapment.

He came back, bent over me, and drew the blanket up to my chin.

"How'd he git caught by the tree?" he asked.

"A squirrelly wind."

Grandpa nodded. Then he gazed up the slope to where Maggie and Tom stood.

As much as his arthritis allowed, Grandpa straightened up and trudged toward the horses. His mouth and chin worked and his face got pinched the way it did when he talked about Grandma. He reached the horses' dragging lines first, and gathered them up. Then he disconnected the doubletree and began to unsnap the buckles on their harnesses. He worked without uttering a sound. He moved up to their heads to unfasten their bridles, and when he was done he stood before them, head bowed. That was all. No nonsense horse talk, no praise, no petting. He clutched his hat in his gnarled old hands and did not lift his head. I don't know what his heart said to those two big horses in those silent moments, but I did know I had no right to watch.

After a moment, Maggie moved to Grandpa and put her muzzle on his shoulder. Then Grandpa took hold of both halters and led the pair across the slope to their rope corral. In the stillness, I could hear water sloshing. He was giving them a saltwater rubdown.

So quietly I could hardly hear his words, Mr. Reynolds said, "Let's go to town. I have to notify Brant's family. I'll radio Ralph at the guard station to pack up your horses and gear. He's a good man with horses."

I was washed up with logging. They'd find a grown man with a team. It didn't matter. After what happened to Brant, I had no heart for the place. I wanted to go home.

No one talked all the way to the cabin. The CB radio scratched, and on the lower hills we heard the booming of sage chickens. That was all. Mr. Reynolds looked sidelong now and then and saw tears starting in my eyes.

When Reynolds stopped at our cabin, he suddenly slapped the steering wheel and blurted, "If only he hadn't looked back to see where the tree was! He must have looked back, or it wouldn't have caught him in the chest! Only a few more feet, a few more feet! and he would have escaped."

"If only he would have stayed away!" I added. "Like I told him to."

Grandpa's voice sounded tired. "If only I hadn't a' let ya go up there."

On the porch, Grandpa ordered, "Go warsh up, Andy. Ya got blood all over ya." He limped to the garden and began harvesting green beans.

I sat on the porch and watched the sun drop behind the mountains. Then I sat in the dark with the radio turned full blast, waiting for news about Brant.

CHAPTER 13

The radio carried no news of Brant until the next morning. Then Grandpa and I heard this report.

"A Forest Service summer employee was critically injured near Bear Mountain yesterday afternoon when a tree fell on him. Brant Jorgeson, nineteen, was working in an area where selective clearing was under way when the wind sent a tree toppling toward him. Jorgeson tried to outrun the tree but it caught him, crushing his chest. His condition at the Eastern Idaho Regional Medical Center is extremely serious."

He'd made it to the hospital. Mr. Reynolds had said if Brant didn't die before he got to the hospital, he might make it.

"Could we go see him, Grandpa? I know you don't like to drive down in the big valley, but . . ."

"Might do. But let's wait till he could know you was there. Could be he'll . . ." Grandpa rubbed his face with his palms. "Well! Let's git our minds on somethin' else. Them horses'll be home taday; let's git busy on that fence."

I heard from both my parents that morning. Dad called from Washington, D.C., to say hi. He asked if I'd like to go hiking the Saturday after he got home. I said no, I didn't feel good.

"You won't be sick three weeks from now, will you, Andy?"

"I think I might be." Just then he got a call on another line, so I didn't have to say any more.

While I was rounding up hammers and nails, the mail carrier brought a letter from Mom. I tore the paper out of the envelope.

Dear Andy,

Working with the horses sounds like lots of fun for you. I hope I can see them in action sometime.

My two summer classes, plus long hours at the insurance company, keep me running. But I've almost earned enough money for my fall tuition. I'm afraid we'll have to postpone your visit. I wish I could afford to send you a bus ticket right now, but that will have to wait until money isn't so tight.

Anyway, Ohio doesn't offer mountains
and fishing. When I get sad about you being
so far away, I remember how much there is
for you to enjoy where you are.

Mom said she'd keep the letter short because
she was exhausted and had to get to bed. I picked
up a pen and started to write her back. But I
didn't know where to start. She didn't know anything about my logging job—I hadn't wanted to
worry her. I crumpled up the paper and looked
out the window. Ohio and Mom seemed a world
away.

In the time I'd been gone, Grandpa had set
posts and tamped them and measured and
notched the poles. Now it was time to nail the
poles to the posts. Driving spike nails with a
sledge was a better job for me than for Grandpa.

Yet, when I picked up the sledge to nail the
pole Grandpa was holding in place, I could barely
lift it. My arms had turned to butter. I let the
hammer slip to the ground, and without saying a
word to Grandpa, I walked down the road.

Peggy Sundstrom was cleaning the counter at
the general store.

"How's your job on the forest?" She grinned.
"I got you that job. Those rangers came in here

wondering where there might be a horse team and . . ."

A smart answer came to mind, but I said, "Thanks, Peggy."

"You owe me a favor, don't you think?"

"What kind?"

"I'd like to go for a ride through town with your horses pulling."

"I don't have a wagon. But someday you could watch . . ." My voice trailed off. I couldn't seem to hold onto a thought any better than I could a hammer.

Peggy was looking at me. "Hey, did you know that guy who got hurt? Dad said he probably was some tinhorn who didn't know his . . ."

I turned and left. For a long while I walked up and down the Dove Valley streets, gazing at the small frame houses with front-yard rock gardens and sprinkler hoses going. I watched Bobby Hodges's mom hanging out a tub of washing in the backyard. When she turned to go into the house, I ducked behind a stop sign.

I walked a mile or so down the highway that leads to Broman's, then turned around and walked back. I sat on the stream bank and picked withered forget-me-nots. What to do next seemed too big a decision for me. So I just sat until my legs got stiff. Then I walked until my feet found the path to the cabin.

Grandpa was wiping his brow with his red handkerchief and resting his arm on a pole he'd just hammered in place when I came up the driveway. The sun was blazing and I knew I should help him. Instead, I shuffled into the house and lay on the sofa.

About three o'clock, Mr. Reynolds drove up in the green vehicle and slowly stepped out. His crisp walk was gone and his uniform was rumpled. I looked down at him from the porch, and his troubled face froze my questions. But he volunteered the information.

"The copter took Brant to the Tower Mountain Clinic. The doctor there inserted a tube in his chest to drain off fluids. Only a few moments more, it would have been too late. After his breathing stabilized, they moved him to the Idaho Falls Hospital."

"So he's going to be all right?"

Mr. Reynolds grimaced. "The lung will heal. But Brant's blood count is falling and the doctors don't know why. They're running tests. Maybe they'll operate. I'll go back down tonight."

"Will he be able to . . . work outdoors and stuff?"

If Brant couldn't play his silly whistle and lug

his nature books around, he wouldn't be Brant.

"Can I go see him?"

"As soon as I know something, I'll call you, Andy."

Maggie and Tom came home soon after Mr. Reynolds left. Ralph, a man with thick black glasses, unloaded them like they were made of china and shyly handed their lead ropes to me. I guess the story of how the horses had rescued Brant must have gotten around on the mountain.

Hugging Maggie around the neck and rubbing Tom's muzzle I whispered, "I'm glad to see you. It's pretty lonely around here."

I put the horses back in Boyd's corral. The realtor still hadn't sold Boyd's cabin—it wasn't modern enough to suit most people. As I fastened the gate behind me, Grandpa growled, "Fer heck's sake! Ain't ya gonna fill the water tub up fer 'em?" Ralph waved good-bye and went back to his truck. I turned and glared at Grandpa. Why did he think he could always talk to me that way?

When Mr. Reynolds called, he sounded tired and worried. Brant's spleen had been injured, he said. In the morning, doctors would operate.

Next morning I ate some biscuits at breakfast and felt my strength returning. When Grandpa picked up his sack of spikes, I followed him out to the fence. I saw him looking at me when I took off my shirt. Like the horses, I'd put on muscle since going to the forest. This time when I picked up the sledge, it felt good to swing it.

I bent the first spike I drove.

"Land Awmighty! Ya think them things don't cost money?" Grandpa shouted in my face. His breath stunk of stale tobacco.

Grandpa tied his pole to the post with a quick, tight knot. I went over to study the knot. I tried to duplicate it on my end, but got the rope tangled.

"Judas! Don't they teach kids nuthin' these days?" Grumbling and cussing, he threw a rope over my end and tied it fast.

When I let a pole slip and it hit Grandpa on the toe, he hollered. "Ya dang clumsy kid!" All at once I felt bone-tired again.

I walked over to Boyd's corral, hung over the fence, and talked to my horses. "I don't know why Grandpa's so grumpy," I told them. "He knows the accident wasn't my fault."

Grandpa and I ate lunch without talking. He gazed out the window, smacking noisily. I thought of my dinners with Brant and how lively and fun they had been. Suddenly I realized something. I hated Grandpa.

I hated his smug silences. I hated it when we were with people he had no use for (and there were lots of them), how he made everyone nervous with his stony-faced silences, like a wolf staring down the rest of the pack. I hated that he didn't care enough about me to ask a polite question—like how was I getting along. Apart from his storytelling, the only talking he did with me was to tell me how stupid I was.

After eating, we went back to work on the fence.

"Good thing ta git this done," Grandpa said. "We'll lose a week o' work gettin' ready fer the fair, then it'll be time fer school."

I looked at him in surprise.

"The *fair*?"

"Yep. It's less'n a month off."

"I don't care anything about the fair now."

"Yeah? Well, they might." He cocked his head toward the horses.

"That's typical." My voice cracked. "For you to worry about how the horses feel and not care a bit about what *I* feel." My voice got louder. "With you, it's always, 'Don't yell at the horses,' 'Don't hit a horse,' 'Don't lose your temper, it hurts their feelings.' You ever think about *my* feelings? I'm a sure enough human being, but do you ever try to be patient with *me*?" I couldn't stop now.

· "Just like the *rest* of them, you are. THEY ALL WANT TO GET ME OUT OF THEIR HAIR. DAD'S SO IMPORTANT, MOM'S SO TIED UP, AND YOU, THEY HAVE TO *PAY* YOU TO KEEP ME. TO ALL OF YOU I'M JUST A . . . JUST . . ." There was a horse pile at my feet. I picked up a horse biscuit and flung it at the fence. "JUST . . . THIS!!"

I picked up another biscuit and another and flung them every which away. "*FAMILY!* I'VE SEEN SAGE CHICKENS THAT HAVE MORE FAMILY THAN I DO. AND THE ONE PERSON WHO TREATED ME BETTER THAN ANYBO . . ." I stopped and looked down at my hands. Manure was smeared all over them. I stomped over to the pump, rammed the handle down hard, and brought up a gush of water. I washed my hands good, then splashed water on the tears running down my face. I started to stalk out of the yard, but I heard a worried voice call, *"Andy!"*

I was scared as Grandpa came toward me. I'd never talked back to him—never had had the nerve. He was limping, but coming along at a steady pace. When he stopped in front of me, his chin was trembling.

"There's truth in what ya say, Andy. I ain't a man ta teach nobody about patience. I ain't got none, except maybe with horses. You're right when ya say I oughta treat muh grandson as good as I treat horses. But I'm ole, and I ain't likely ta change.

"But one thing ya said ain't true—not a bit. I ain't never took one nickel ta keep care o' ya. Your dad, Linden, he don't understand these things. I told 'im and told 'im I didn't want no part o' his money. But the checks kept acomin', so I started puttin' 'em away fer ya. I didn't know what ya'd ever need the money fer; your Dad has plenty. Then this summer I had an idee. I wanted ta keep it a surprise till we finished up this fence, but I might as well tell ya. I bought Old Boyd's wagon fer ya."

I squinted up at the bright sky. I couldn't believe it. He'd bought Boyd's wagon for me!

"But I realize, things has changed. Ya don't have ta mess with the horses er drive that wagon till ya want ta. If that's never, that's awright. Ya think I don't know that was real tough fer ya the other day? Judas, I ain't slept a wink, blamin' muhself and thinkin' how that coulda been you under a tree. I don't know how ta say things right, so I don't say 'em atall. But in here," he patted his chest, "in here I knowed that was hard on ya."

He shuffled away a few steps. Then he stopped.

"About your folks. I don't understand 'em neither. It ain't natural fer 'em to see so little of ya.
But it happens. Happens with ducks and cows
and sheep and horses. Ya saw how old Tom's
mama didn't pay no attention to 'im? Weren't *his*
fault. And it ain't yours neither."

I stood there a long time. I thought about the
things I'd said and the things Grandpa had said.
Maybe I should have been sorry. Instead I felt
like a sack of grain had slipped off my shoulders.
I thought about the wagon I'd wanted so bad and
was surprised to find that something in me still
wanted it.

I walked over and took the sledge away from
Grandpa. "Here, I'll do this."

We made a lot of progress on the fence during
the afternoon. I wondered if Mr. Reynolds might
be trying to call, but I knew I couldn't park myself beside the phone and fret.

I began to see that summer would go on. I'd
fish and play ball with Bobby Hodges. I'd like the
wagon—I hadn't had a chance to just have fun
with my horses. I'd take Peggy Sundstrom on
that ride she'd wanted. Grandpa and I probably
would go back to scheming and dreaming about
the fair and the Labor Day pulling contest. We'd
get our fence built, with Grandpa still yelling at
me. In all ways you could see, everything would

go on as before. Even though Brant's accident had changed the inside of me. The nicest guy I'd ever known had almost died right before my eyes. But I hadn't fallen to pieces until afterward—I'd done my best to help.

Later in the day, the sun turned gray and the wind kicked up. Lightning zipped across the valley and thunder rumbled. "They're movin' spud wagons up there," Grandpa said.

When it began to rain, it fell in buckets. For hours the sky sparkled and thunder roared. Our electricity was knocked out. Grandpa lit some candles and settled on the sofa with a *Reader's Digest*. I went to bed. When the phone rang, I stumbled through the dark, groped for the receiver, and grabbed it.

"The surgery was a complete success," Mr. Reynolds said. "When Brant awoke this afternoon, he already looked better." I held out the receiver so Grandpa could hear, too. "The doctors look for a complete recovery. Considering how close he came to dying, it's amazing he'll be released in a few days. Then he'll go home to Illinois. He'll need to rest for a couple months."

Grandpa took the receiver from me. His bony old hand trembled.

"BOB. THANKS FER CALLIN' ME 'N' ANDY WITH THAT GOOD WORD."

CHAPTER 14

"Who's gonna help you hookin' up at the contest?" Bobby asked.

It was Saturday, the day before Grandpa and I were to leave for the fair, and I was giving Tom a bath with the hose. Bobby's voice sounded casual, but when I peered around at him, his face was hopeful. I'd been thinking Bobby could help Grandpa hook the doubletree to the stoneboat and then move out of the way fast, and I'd been planning to ask him to be part of my fair crew. But something had come up to change things.

"Wellington Boyd came home and I think I better ask him," I said. "He's old, you know."

" 'Bout ten years older'n God. He won't have many more chances, all right. How come Old Man Boyd came back?"

"He thought it'd be great to live in an Arizona

apartment house with lots of old people. But it turned out he and the rest didn't have much to say to each other."

"He probably scared 'em off."

"He thought he'd like not pulling weeds and fixing fences, but he missed it. And he hated the heat. One night at ten-thirty, he decided he'd had all he could stand and packed up his things and left right then. Grandpa said Old Man Boyd didn't even wait to have his deposits refunded. He must have been desperate!"

"Good thing he still had his place here. Well, let me know if there's anything I can do to help you. Our family is going down on Monday. Mom says she hasn't been so excited about the fair since she was little."

Reed Sundstrom had offered to carry my horses to Blackfoot. He was taking a dairy exhibit and he had extra space in his stock truck. Dairy exhibits had to be checked in on Sunday, so Mr. Sundstrom was picking up Maggie and Tom early next day. Grandpa was glad the horses would have a full day to get used to the noises and smells of the fairgrounds. Grandpa had decided we'd go down in the pickup so we could sleep in it Sunday night. Old Man Boyd said he'd come down on Monday. Now that he was back home, he wasn't about to sleep any more nights in foreign places. The pulling contest started at 4 P.M.

Saturday morning I walked down to the general store to pick up some cookies and peanuts for the trip. Hanging across the front porch was an old sheet, with GOOD LUCK, ANDY, written with markers. It looked like everyone in town had signed it. I wondered if that would make Reed Sundstrom feel bad—he took a dairy exhibit to the state fair every year, and no one had ever made a banner for him. But I suppose he understood that the dairy show only attracted milk-cow raisers, and the horse pull attracted everyone.

Sunday morning Mr. Sundstrom came over early to load Maggie and Tom.

"I figure it's okay for me to miss church once a year." He glanced around guiltily as he spoke.

"Ya kin miss a lot more'n once and it won't bother me none," Grandpa said.

I took hold of my horses' halters and led them in behind Sundstrom's bathed and gleaming cows. Then the big truck with the lettering SUND-STROM'S FINEST QUALITY MILK, DOVE VALLEY, IDAHO, pulled away. As soon as it did, Grandpa and I jumped into his old pickup and headed for Blackfoot.

Our road wound above a sky-blue lake where

swans were swimming, cut through granite hills, and finally dropped into a green river valley.

"Look at them quakies." Grandpa pointed at an aspen grove. "Already golden. Winter ain't that fer away."

I was wishing he'd watch the snaking highway. I asked, in an innocent way, how the song about Nellie went, though I knew it so well I could have hummed it in my sleep. Grandpa began to sing.

"I kicked Nelly in the belly in the baaaaaaarn, 'Cause the old man said it wouldn't do no haaaarm. . . ."

"Grandpa," I asked, "Maggie and Tom have a good chance, don't they? They moved that boulder."

"That mighta been a fluke. Them two coulda sensed it was life er death. And we don't know how they'll take to a fair. Fer as this contest goes, they're plumb green."

When we pulled up at the empty fairgrounds, I could hardly figure out where we were. I'd only seen Blackfoot when the fair was in progress and cars lined the main street for dozens of blocks and open-sided buses drove around collecting pedestrians.

Grandpa wanted to make sure everything

about our entry was in order, so he headed for
the fair office. I wandered down the empty midway. No Ferris wheel blinked its lights overhead,
no screams from the Dragon Ride carried down
the walkways, and food booths were boarded
shut. The quietness put me on edge—I wanted
the fair to sound and smell like a familiar place.

Suddenly a black truck pulling a horse trailer
swerved onto the roadway and almost hit me. Its
driver laid on the horn and the blast made me
jump for the lawn. The truck barreled toward
the horse stalls. On its side was painted a fancy
white and red sign.

SCOURMAN'S MIGHTY SHIRES

I'd heard of Scourman—everyone in Eastern
Idaho had. He was a potato millionaire and the
owner of a fertilizer plant. He even owned race-
horses. When people in Idaho wanted to say
someone had big wealth, they'd say, "He's rich as
Scourman."

I watched a sandy-haired kid back horses out
of the Scourman trailer. I gasped. Their coats
gleamed with health, their white feathers were
combed and shiny. They tossed their heads and
their nostrils quivered.

"Hey, I been lookin' fer ya!" Grandpa came up beside me. "Figgered ya was swallered up by a ..." His gaze went to the black rig. "Holy Moses! There's ole Buck Scourman hisself."

In body type, Scourman matched the horses. He was a huge man—tall, with wide shoulders and back. Except the horses were working fit, and Scourman's belly hung over his wide, turquoise belt, and a thick, black beard hid his face.

"You know him?"

"We've met up. But he wouldn't remember me. I knowed 'im when he was a big awk'ard kid workin' fer 'is pa. In them days he could shake windas when he laughed. But he got hard and sour on the way ta gittin' rich."

"You think he trained that team?"

"Phhh! He don't know nothin' 'bout horses. He's hired someone to train 'em er bought a experienced team."

"The prize money isn't worth it."

"Fer Scourman, it'd be the chance ta be top dog at one more thing."

"Maybe he can't drive good."

Grandpa shrugged.

"Can we go meet him and look at the horses?"

"Later. Let's find where Reed put our two. He might be adoin' our work fer us." He folded up a piece of paper. "Tamorry, startin' at seven A.M., they'll weigh in the horses. Let's hope Maggie and Tom go as lightweights."

Maggie and Tom didn't shine like Scourman's black Shires. They weren't as tall and their muscles didn't stretch against their hide, but Grandpa and I were really glad to see them stalled and munching hay. They looked up and nickered. We'd only been separated for a few hours, but it seemed like days.

A short man with a round pink face came around the corner. I recognized him as Roy "Uncle Chatty" Chatlosh. He was eighty-five that year but he strode toward Grandpa with a brisk walk and a wide, near toothless smile.

"Eldro Pendrey! I seen your name on the list in the office. So you're down with a team this year! That makes me glad I ain't." He smiled my way, and his eyes disappeared into layers of wrinkles.

"Chatty, ya know I ain't fit ta plow in your dust. It's muh grandson here 'at's takin' the team—I only paid the check. Me 'n' Wellington Boyd, we're gonna be 'is hookers."

Uncle Chatty drew close and looked up at me. "You as good a hand with horses as your granddad?"

Grandpa answered. "He pulled a feed wagon

fer a sheep outfit up our way this summer, and
he skidded logs up on the forest. That tell ya
somethin'?"

Uncle Chatty fairly beamed. "It does me good
ta hear! I love ta see kids usin' horses, not just fer
shows and winnin' ribbons. Tell me about your
horses, son."

We moved to the horses' heads.

"This is Maggie. She's real honest and strong.
She's got lots of heart, and Grandpa says she's as
good as the best mare he ever had."

Uncle Chatty absently stroked her head. His
eyes were on me.

"This is Tom. He's a clown. Always looking
to play a joke. He loves a good time, but he's
real smart and if you had to, you could trust your
life . . ." I stopped. Unexpectedly, the memory of
Brant's accident washed over me. I leaned my
forehead against Tom's face and couldn't say a
word more.

Uncle Chatty was nodding and saying, "Uh-
huh, uh-huh." Then he turned to the horses. He
studied them awhile. He moved Tom's forelock
aside. "Yep. Nice high sworl. He's smart."

He did the same to Maggie. "Smart, you bet.
Don't come no smarter."

I wanted him to look over the rest of them and
tell me if their shoulders and rumps looked like

they could win a pulling contest. But Grandpa interrupted.

"Tell me you're pullin' muh leg, Chatty, about not bringin' down a team this year."

"It's the God's truth. Two weeks ago a man outa Warshington called, wantin' ta buy a team. I told 'im I had one agoin' good, but I didn't want ta sell it. I put a price on 'em sa high I thought the man would hang up on me. But he said, okay, I'll be after 'em. When a man'll pay that kind o' money, ya gotta take it. It'll pay the feed bill on the others I got comin' up."

"I'm sure glad you don't have a team in this year, Uncle Chatty, but those big Shires scare me."

"Scourman's!" The smile left the old man's face. "He showed up at a pull in Montana last month."

"How'd he do?"

"He won. Broke the rules. His hooker poked the horses on the shoulder with a nail. I don't know why them judges didn't disqualify 'im."

"Ya figger they was in 'is pocket?"

"Nope, I don't think. Folks is so good ta go by the rules, them judges git lazy and fergit ta be watchin'."

"Scourman got a good team?"

"A good team! Hate ta see a team that good in

the hands of a man who'll do anythin' ta win. My boy Dennis has a racehorse and he's seen the ignernt things Scourman has pulled in racin'! Not quite illegal—just ignernt. Let's go find us a cup o' coffee, Eldro. Want anythin' Andy?"

"No. I'll stay here."

I crawled up on the stall's gate, stretched out my legs across the top pole, and leaned back against the gatepost. I pulled a package of cheese and crackers out of my shirt pocket. I was so absorbed in spreading cheese on a cracker, I didn't hear anyone come up. When all at once I became aware of a great figure beside me, I lost my balance and tumbled off the gate into the straw. Buck Scourman's dark frame towered above me.

"Who does this pair of Percherons belong to?" His voice sounded like echoes off a canyon wall.

"They're mine." I wanted to sound proud, but it came out like a mouse squeak.

"This pair ain't in the pullin' contest?"

"Yeah, they are."

"These horses full growed?"

"Yeah!"

He nodded and his mouth pulled down in a smirk.

"I'm just goin' around lookin' at the competition." He walked on.

I knew it wouldn't be good to hang around the barn all afternoon stewing the insults, so I wandered through a building where women were hanging up quilts for display and arranging bread and cookies and rolls in a glass case. I strolled through the art building and tried to look at photos of brides and little kids.

I couldn't take any interest in the paintings either. I went out to the midway and for a while watched carnies setting up games and tables and assembling rides. One young guy turning bolts on the Scrambler didn't look sober. A truck drove up with a white-and-green sign that had a laughing face on it and the word FREAKS.

I was walking toward the dairy barn to see if I could find Mr. Sundstrom and Peggy when I noticed right ahead of me, beside a big combine on display, Buck Scourman talking to Uncle Chatty. I never meant to eavesdrop—I only slipped behind the machine to avoid more ridicule from Scourman. But Scourman's conversation stopped me there.

"You're the man to judge, Chatlosh. You've seen my team. Who could beat it?"

I peered around the combine's great tire. Beside the small, pink-faced Uncle Chatty, Scourman looked even more mammoth.

"Ya got a good team, awright, Scourman. But

Bud Rose's from Rexburg is keen. Laron Fielding from Alpine is keen and so is Dell Summers from Utah. Still, fer my money, the team ya'll have ta beat is Eldro and Andy Pendrey from Dove Valley."

Scourman threw back his head and roared like a waterfall. Two women carrying notebooks turned to look at him.

"Who're ya kiddin'? A gimpy old man, a green kid, and a pair of puny grays? You see somethin' in 'em *I* can't!"

Uncle Chatty wagged a stubby finger at the giant. "It *ain't* nuthin' ta see! It's somethin' ya just feel."

"Is that right? And just what is that, Chatlosh?"

"It's called love. And it wins contests."

I thought the big man would probably split apart laughing at that idea. Instead, his brows dove to his nose. He slammed his hat back on his head, pushed a cowboy aside, and strode off toward his rig.

It wasn't the sight of his huge back that intimidated me—it was something I'd seen on his face when he stormed past. Something that made me wish Uncle Chatty hadn't identified Maggie and Tom as the team to beat.

CHAPTER 15

At dinnertime, Grandpa wanted us to load up with a big restaurant meal so we'd sleep soundly that night and not fret the next day's contest. Grandpa and I wandered down Blackfoot's sleepy main street looking for a place to eat. I spied a Chinese restaurant and started to go in. Grandpa hung back.

"I like ta know what I'm eatin'," he said. "There's a lot o' wiggly things in Chinese dishes 'at I don't recognize."

"I'm starving," I pleaded.

Reluctantly, Grandpa followed. After the Chinese host had settled us at a table, Grandpa peered around the room. The tables were filled with men wearing cowboy hats or billed caps lettered with the names of farm-equipment manufacturers.

"See, Grandpa? The place is full. The food must be fine."

"Pa said them Chinese 'at worked the mines up at Caribou City used ta eat dogs."

"That was a long time ago! There're laws against that now." I was wishing Grandpa wouldn't talk so loud.

A petite Chinese waitress came up and asked our order. Grandpa stared at her so long I grew embarrassed and hastily ordered the Sunday special for both of us.

After she left Grandpa hissed, "Did ya see the hands on that girl? They was smaller'n a kindy-gartner's. Good thing she works in a Chinese restaurant. Them hands wouldn't hardly fit around a big bakin' potata." I moved my chair and peered out the window, hoping it would seem like I wasn't with Grandpa. I was sure everyone in both dining rooms could hear him.

When the girl delivered our food, Grandpa peered over the table at her feet.

"Yep!" he cried as she moved toward the kitchen. "Feet're the same way. Little as sheep hooves. Ya couldn't depend on 'em ta take ya no distance atall. In a horse, I like a substantial foot. Used ta have a geldin' with feet like dishpans. I could git on that horse 'n' travel . . ." I was so anxious to get out of there I wolfed down my food without tasting it. Grandpa stayed so busy rubbernecking and commenting about people at the tables, he barely got to his dinner. The waitress put our leftovers in little cardboard cartons and we left.

Back at the fairgrounds, Grandpa went off to find his cronies. I washed up at the faucet behind the horse barn, then stopped to feed and water Maggie and Tom and say good night.

"Tomorrow's the big day," I told them. I combed their forelocks with my fingers. "Those bleachers will be packed. The Shires look tough, but we know something, don't we? That you've got what it takes."

I needed a good night's sleep, but I was too antsy to crawl into my sleeping bag yet. I wandered up a dark path to the livestock barns. In the dairy barn, cows and bulls were bedded down, chewing their cuds with eyes closed. I looked for the Sundstroms, but no owners were still around.

I walked through to the 4-H building and saw a blond-headed girl about nine asleep in a stall beside two sleeping lambs. Why was I so restless? As I walked out of the barn, something made me turn onto a footpath leading to the camper parking area. I realized then where my hunch was taking me. I had to find Grandpa.

Almost at once, I came upon a group of men seated in lawn chairs behind a camper. Grandpa was among them. In the midst of the group, a couple of men were setting up a card table. Silhouetted in a lantern's glow was the towering figure of Buck Scourman. His voice boomed.

"Yessir, we'll all be competing against each other tomorrow; no reason not to get to know each other tonight. I say there's no better way to get acquainted than over a friendly game of poker."

Two old men in bib overalls got up.

"Count us out," one said. "We ain't gamblers. See you gentlemen tomorrow."

A young guy I recognized as Laron Fielding, who always brought over a good team from Wyoming, pulled a chair to the table. Grandpa did, too. So did Scourman, and a fourth man named Roland Harrop. Two others stood beside the table. Scourman produced a deck of cards and handed them to Fielding, who shuffled and cut them. Then Scourman reached behind his chair and pulled out of his coat a bottle of whiskey and plastic glasses. I knew he was up to something.

"I guess we ought to make this real friendly,"

he chuckled. In the glow of the lantern I could see his coyote smile. He was grinning at Grandpa, eyebrows raised. Grandpa pushed his glass forward and Scourman began to pour. Scourman glanced at the man I didn't know and winked. He was going to try to get Grandpa drunk.

I stepped from behind the tree and made my way to Grandpa's elbow. Scourman narrowed his eyes when he saw me.

"Grandpa," I said, "it's late. Aren't you coming to bed?"

"Not fer a while." He saw me staring at the drink beside his wrist. "You go on—I'll be along later, Andy."

"Grandpa. It wouldn't be a . . . good thing . . . for you to stay up." I saw Laron Fielding put down his cards and look at me in sympathy.

"Your grandson might be right, Eldro. Maybe we all need sleep more than we need a poker game?" He looked hopefully at the others.

Scourman was immobile, except for his eyes which found my face. They were cold, dead eyes.

Grandpa looked at me, too, with a hard, warning scowl.

"This don't concern ya, Andy. You git now."

Didn't concern me? I needed him fit and alert the next day! That was like Brant telling me to mind my own business about cutting trees which might try to smash and kill him. No one ever wanted to listen to a kid, even when he was right.

In front of those men, I couldn't beg him not to start drinking. I stalked away from the table and toward the parking area. I strode past the truck, so mad I could hardly see, past the midway, past the fair offices, and out the gates. Two long-haired Native Americans from the Fort Hall Reservation stared at me. I glared back.

Grandpa and I had always planned that I'd drive at the contest, but he'd be right there with advice. There was a lot about strategy I didn't know. Despite how well I got along with the horses, I'd only make a fool of myself to try to be in the contest without Grandpa. Couldn't Grandpa see Scourman wanted him to have a hangover the next day? How could he choose whiskey over our big chance? I was walking so fast I'd gobbled up two city blocks already.

When I remembered the banner at Pat's General Store, my anger turned to sadness. The people in Dove Valley were expecting a good performance in the arena tomorrow. I didn't have to win, but I wanted to make a good showing. Even fourth place paid $200—that was a darn nice prize. Could I hope to do well without Grandpa's help? Could someone like Uncle Chatty step in and give me a hand?

I'd walked a lot farther than I'd meant to. When I turned around, I couldn't even see the fairgrounds. But I was glad, in a way, because as I walked back I grew drowsy. I wondered if I would sleep any, feeling unbuttoned like I did. But when I found the truck, I crawled into my sleeping bag and fell asleep.

I woke up at dawn. I stretched and remembered what day it was. The disappointment of the night before was still with me. I shoved my elbow against a stick poking me in the back. Something moaned.

Grandpa, in his sleeping bag, rolled over and muttered, "What'd ya hit me fer?"

"What are *you* doing here?"

"This is my pickup, and I'm asleepin' in it 'cause it's drier'n sleepin' on the ground. But I mighta took the ground had I knowed you was gonna bruise me up this mornin'."

"But . . . I thought . . . last night . . ."

"Ya took me fer dumb, like Scourman did, huh? Thought I couldn't tell he was up ta one o' his ignernt tricks?"

"Uncle Chatty had told him you and I were the guys to beat, that's why he was after you."

"Even if Chatty hadn'ta told 'im we was the team ta watch, he's been in business long enough ta sense who 'is competition is."

"But you took the whiskey. I saw you hold out your glass."

"I took it. But that don't mean I drunk it. I guess I still know a trick er two about gittin' rid of a drink without drinkin' it. The ole timber buyers used ta do that to us. Figgered they'd git us mountain boys drunk an' we'd sign our logs away fer cheap. But we fooled 'em a time er two. Watched 'em git theirselves pickled, then we suggested talkin' business."

He chuckled. "Ole Scourman, he sure did look surprised last night when I stood up, sober as a owl, after all the drinks he'd been a pourin'. Laron Fielding, he just grinned, but Scourman and Roland Harrop, they was kinda beewildered."

"Scourman will be mad today. It'll get around you made a fool of him."

"He made a fool of hisself." Grandpa lifted himself up on his elbows and looked at me. "I wouldn'ta started drinkin' if muh best friend had offered it." He waited a moment. "Ya think I'd want ta be the one o' the four 'at couldn't be counted on?"

I'd never admit to him I'd wondered if I might have to find a replacement for him.

We rolled up our sleeping bags, then fed the horses.

"Let's go warsh the dust off 'em, before the hose gits busy. Then we'll git some cinnamon rolls. An' we got leftover subgum and egg food stuff to go with it."

We were standing in line to weigh our team when Wellington Boyd arrived. He was cussing and storming because the man at the gate had charged him admission.

"I tole 'im I was part of the show taday, but he charged me anyways. I says to 'im, 'How much money ya make on that pullin' contest? Plenty! An' still ya wanta take advantage of a ole pensioner whose gonna be a hooker taday!' " Suddenly Old Man Boyd spied the big Scourman Shires. He forgot his complaint.

"Judas!" he gasped. "Where'd *they* come from?"

"Scourman brought a team this year!"

"Scourman? *Buck* Scourman? He ain't inta draft horses!"

"He is now."

"Well, Eldro, ya kin awwus hope them Shires don't end up in yer weight class."

Scourman weighed in just ahead of us. The sandy-haired kid, whom Scourman yelled at a lot, led the first great horse into the boxlike platform scale. It weighed 1,708.

Grandpa hit Boyd on the shoulder.

"Yihoo! Double that, 'n' Scourman'll be in the heavyweight and we won't have ta worry about 'im."

"Look how ganted up that horse is, Eldro. Bet Scourman ain't fed and watered 'im for eighteen hours."

The kid led the second black onto the scale. It weighed 1,582. I quickly added the numbers in my head. Cutoff for the middleweight division was 3,300 pounds. Scourman's team weighed 3,290—he was in the middleweights. The sandy-haired kid led the Shires off to get food and water into them.

Scourman watched with narrowed eyes while I led Tom onto the scale. He weighed 1,402. Grandpa winked at me when I handed Tom to him. Lightweight division ended at 2,900 pounds—we had a good chance of making it. I led Maggie onto the scale. My stomach hurt as the fair officials fiddled the metal weights.

"Fifteen hundred on the nose," he announced. I added the numbers. We were two pounds into the middleweight division. I saw a malevolent smirk on Scourman's face.

Old Man Boyd scolded Grandpa on the way back to the barn.

"Eldro, ya shouldn'ta give 'em no food and water till after the weigh-in!"

"They awwus eat early."

"One day in the year, they can't have breakfast late? Only two pounds! Ya coulda avoided them Shires altagether."

"Mighta done. But now I think about it, it might be a good thing ta be in the middleweights. Feels ta me like that's where the action's gonna be."

CHAPTER 16

Grandpa stood beside the barn and squinted at a crumpled sheet of paper. On it he'd written the names of men who would compete in the middleweight division.

"Looka here," he sighed, "with the exception o' Scourman, there ain't a man here ya wouldn't be proud ta lose ta. These men're teamsters."

He limped to a bench and eased himself onto it. "Thane Kinghorn from Bone. He's the thin serious feller, got the nice pair o' blond Belgians. Max Smith from Blackfoot—good man, ain't too experienced though. Bud Rose from Rexburg—a big Percheron and a roan Belgian. Fielding from Alpine—a helluva man with horses. Dell Summers from Utah, got a team in ever' division and they'll *all* be keen. With our team and Scourman's, that makes seven teams."

His voice sounded tired, but when he looked up, his eye held a sparkle.

"Wouldn't that be a feather in our bonnets, ta beat competition like *that*?"

He pulled his tarnished pocket watch from his overalls and looked at it.

"Three o'clock. Ya ever seen a day drag by so? Let's go over by the arena and visit with the others. Might as well be stewin' there as here. Fill up them buckets and bring 'em—it's liable to git thirsty later. I'll take the horses."

When I reached the arena, I took the horses' lead ropes from Grandpa and walked Maggie and Tom around on the grass. People started to come by.

Loretta Hodges and Bobby stood next to the fence separating the racetrack from the lawn and waved. Bobby's mom insisted on reaching through and touching the horses' necks.

"Good luck, Maggie. Good luck, Tom." She caught my wrist and squeezed it. "Andy. *Good* luck." Her eyes were moist.

"She cries over everything," Bobby muttered. Loretta turned to get a tissue from her purse. Bobby put on a weepy face, grabbed my wrist, and whispered in a squeaky voice, "*Good* luck."

Reed Sundstrom walked over from the dairy barns and shook first Grandpa's hand, then mine. "Do us proud, Andy."

Peggy offered advice. "Don't get nervous, because if you do, the horses will feel it and get nervous, too." I wondered how it was Peggy felt she could advise on subjects she knew nothing about. But it didn't annoy me quite like it used to.

Laron Fielding came by and wished me luck—then one by one other competitors stopped by to shake my hand. I was too embarrassed to remember to tell them good luck, too. Scourman hadn't shown up with his pair of Shires yet, and the lightweight division pull was about to get under way.

Wellington Boyd clumped over, and though he stood only a foot away, hollered, "It's too hot fer them colts o' yours ta be pullin' taday!" I knew whether it'd been warm or cool, windy or calm, it wouldn't have seemed to him to be a good day for pulling.

Restless, I walked the horses around on the grass again. I saw a tall man, a sore thumb in pressed pants and gleaming shoes, crossing the track and walking toward me. I could hardly believe it. It was Dad.

"You're here?" I asked stupidly.

"Obviously. I didn't go to Germany. I sent Johnson to present my paper."

"Why?"

"Sunday afternoon, I stopped in Dove Valley at Pat's General Store. I saw the banner hanging there and I realized this is a big event. A man ought to be able to escape work long enough to watch his boy, huh?"

I wanted to say, "Thanks for coming," but the words got stuck. "Good luck, Andy," Dad said.

They'd finished clearing the grandstands of people who'd been watching the 4-H Horse Show. Now they were admitting those with tickets for the horse pulling. People filled the lower rows first—then they began to pick their way to the higher bleachers. Soon the stands were crammed.

The five lightweight teams moved onto the tracks and paraded in front of the grandstand. The teamsters were Bud Rose, a man named Jenkins, Dell Summers, wearing a new red shirt under his coveralls, Roland Harrop, one of the men I'd seen with Scourman at the poker game, and Dan Wilson, the owner of a team of Fjords, miniature draft horses. The Fjords got the biggest applause.

The teams returned to the waiting area. A truck pulled onto the track and a crew wearing

Eastern Idaho State Fair shirts loaded 100-pound sacks onto the stoneboat, until the sled bore 2,350 pounds.

Rose was the first to pull, and his team moved the boat ten feet with ease. Harrop was next. He took his lines in hand and yelled, "HEY-UP, HEY-UP," and his red horses walked off effortlessly.

Next to pull were the small Fjords. The announcer explained that unlike other horses, the Fjords did not like quiet when they were pulling. They liked encouragement. It took the crowd a couple of pulls to get used to this breach of pulling-contest etiquette, but by the time the teams began to struggle with their loads, the crowd had taught itself to cheer and yell for the Fjords and still remain quiet for the big teams. The crowd liked the Fjords, and every time the little blonds trotted into place, spectators whistled and hooted, "Come on, Shorty!" When the Fjords pulled 5,000 pounds, the crowd applauded happily.

On the next pull, Bud Rose dropped out. His black gelding, Rube, was favoring a front leg. The crowd gave him a nice hand as Rose walked his team to the trailer area.

With Rose out, Harrop moved into the number one slot. That meant he decided how much weight

was added. Rose had been trying to keep the
Fjords in the contest by adding only 500
pounds each pull. But Harrop upped the load
by 1,000 pounds. That stuck the Fjords on their
next turn.

So none of us were disappointed when Harrop
went outside the rope barrier, disqualifying himself on that pull. He tried again at the end of the
round, but could only persuade his team to pull
the stoneboat eight feet. Teams had to go the full
ten feet to qualify for the next pull. Summers
and Jenkins did pull the full distance.

On the next try, with 7,500 on the stoneboat,
Jenkins made three attempts. His longest pull
was six and a half feet. Then it was Dell Summers's turn. On his first pull the horses didn't
budge it; the second try he pulled three feet. His
hookers unhooked him, and Summers walked his
horses in a wide circle, then returned. That time
he pulled eight feet to win the lightweight division.

Summers dusted off his red shirt, jumped onto
his doubletree, and rode round the track, lifting
his billed hat. The crowd was still applauding
Summers when suddenly Scourman's team trotted onto the track. You could almost hear the
crowd catch its breath. Since morning, those two
Shires had been fed and watered good. Their

black coats gleamed from hair spray, their snowy ankle feathers were bathed and combed and red ribbons were braided into their tails. They looked more ready to compete in a parade than a working class, but the crowd loved their flashy appearance and cheered as the Shires pranced before the stands. Scourman turned a grateful smile to them. Now I knew why Scourman hadn't been around earlier—he wanted the attention of a late, grand entrance.

Grandpa came up beside me. "The announcer ain't even asked fer middleweight horses ta parade yet, but look at that fool, asoakin' up the limelight."

Uncle Chatty came up wearing a smile that buried his eyes in folds of wrinkles.

"I was over ta the fair office and they give me somethin' to give ya."

He handed me a yellow Western Union envelope. I started to rip it open and was surprised to see my hands were trembling. Scourman's appearance on the track had shaken me.

I unfolded the paper and read it.

ANDY GOOD LUCK TODAY STOP I MISS YOU AND THE HORSES STOP SHOW EVERYBODY WHO'S BEST STOP I AM FEELING GOOD STOP BRANT

I read the message twice, then folded the paper over and over into a yellow cube and stuck it in my shirt pocket for good luck. The announcer had called for the middleweight teams to parade by the grandstand, and Grandpa and Uncle Chatty were nagging at me to get going.

That morning I'd drawn a 7—last place. I'd pull after Scourman, who'd drawn a 6.

Dell Summers was in the number one slot. The crowd was pleased to see the man in the red shirt back with another team. Max Smith from Blackfoot was next, and was welcomed like a hometown contestant should be. Thane Kinghorn from Bone, a man who played banjo for a living and whose horses looked as solemn-eyed as he, was next. Bud Rose returned with his second team, then came Laron Fielding, smiling behind his team like he was having the best time in the world. The crowd liked that and cheered for him.

But the loudest applause came for Scourman, who paraded his beautiful team past a second time. I was to follow Scourman, but I dropped my lines in the dirt, fumbled to gather them up, and ended up running behind Maggie and Tom, who were trying to catch up with the other horses.

I only wanted to pass by as inconspicuously as

possible, but two things prevented that. First, in about the eighth row of bleachers, a big white sheet suddenly was lifted up. It was the one that had hung in Pat's General Store and its big letters shouted GOOD LUCK, ANDY. I wanted to pretend that banner wasn't for me, but I knew if I did I'd get it from Grandpa. So I transferred the lines to one hand, fearing I might drop them again, and waved feebly with the other.

Then the announcer started in.

"Ladies and Gentlemen. It's a pleasure to introduce this team. In my years of announcing here, we've never had a competitor as young as this one. Andy Pendrey from Dove Valley, Idaho. Andy and his grandpa trained this young team of Percherons and brought them down today to be part of our famous Eastern Idaho State Fair Pulling Contest.

"We read so much about the other kind of youth—those on drugs, those backsassing their elders—and then there're kids like this. All of us who admire horses know that horses and good citizenship go together."

I wanted to shrink up and disappear. The crowd clapped, but it seemed to me they'd used up their energy in cheering for Scourman.

I went back to the gate to wait my first turn. Uncle Chatty walked up and grinned at me.

"Lot o' folks're behind ya, Andy. Includin' me."
He squeezed my shoulder and winked.

The loading crew pulled up in their white truck
and loaded 2,950 pounds onto the boat. Dell
Summers rolled up the sleeves on his bright red
shirt and ambled over to the boat. After his
horses were in position he called out, in a matter-
of-fact voice, "Jenny, Jen-ny," to the mare half of
his team and the boat slid ten feet and uprooted
the flag.

Max Smith from Blackfoot walked his pair of
Shires to the boat. They were lighter boned and
not gussied up like Scourman's, but they were tall
and stylish nonetheless. Someone in the stands
called, "C'mon, Blackfoot!" Smith's Shires pulled
the load handily, but something about the way
Smith handled himself looked amateurish.

Thane Kinghorn, the banjo player from Bone,
looked like he'd lost his best friend as he moved
to the stoneboat. His horses had ragged coats
with a skiff of road dust on them and, waiting for
the hookers to connect them up, they looked as
sad-eyed as their owner. But when Kinghorn told
them to pull, they almost ran away with the boat.

"Holy Moses!" Grandpa muttered. "He's
gonna be tough!"

Laron Fielding, smiling behind his team of big
browns, sauntered into position. The horses

seemed not to notice the boat behind them as they walked away. Then came Bud Rose's big gray and blocky roan, and they too pulled easily.

Huge applause greeted Scourman and his flashy Shires. Scourman turned to the stands with a smile to accept the applause, but there was something behind his grin that seemed like contempt. That may have been where he began to lose favor with the crowd. Or it may have been the way he spat orders at Harrop and the sandy-haired kid as they backed the team into position.

Scourman yelled, *"GIT UP!"* the sled glided off, and the red flag sprung out of the ground.

They'd all made it look so easy, my only worry as I walked to the stoneboat was that Grandpa and Wellington Boyd might not get out of the way quick enough after they hooked me up. After all, they had arthritis, and stooping over might give them catches in their backs. And Maggie and Tom would be in a big hurry to pull.

So it struck me dumb when they failed to move that easy load. I called "Maggie, Tom," and they edged forward in a halfhearted way, but stopped when they felt the weight of the boat. That counted as a try, of course—it was a try whenever the teamster spoke to the team.

Grandpa looked at me in alarm, said we'd unhook and go around and try again. I followed the horses and my two hookers in a circle while my mind raced. What if they failed on the first load? What could I find to blame it on? What would I say to the two rows of fans from Dove Valley?

Grandpa and Wellington Boyd hooked me up again. "No-good twin-borns." Old Man Boyd scolded. That time Maggie and Tom pulled the ten feet. Yet unlike the previous teams, they acted like it was a big load. I returned to the gate and demanded of Uncle Chatty, "What's wrong with them?"

"Maybe they just ain't warmed up."

Everyone went for their second try. Except for Smith, who seemed to lack experience in handling his team, the drivers again moved the load like it was made of feathers. Then it was my turn. Maggie and Tom failed to pull it on the first try. We stayed hooked up, and tried again. Tom crowded against Maggie and tried to bite her. When I called her name, Maggie didn't flick an ear and lumbered forward only a few feet. The officials measured—I'd pulled four feet.

We unhooked and circled the horses. Grandpa and Old Man Boyd hooked them up quick, so they'd scarcely notice they'd been attached to the boat, and that time they dragged it ten feet.

"What's wrong with them!" I demanded of Grandpa.

"They're Percherons, and smart. Mebbe they're scoffin' at that size load." He didn't sound convinced.

Dell Summers ordered the load increased by 1,000. He'd increased by only 500 pounds the first time, probably to give me a break and let my horses warm up. But after my second bleak try, I think he decided it'd be kinder to eliminate me as soon as possible.

I would have done anything rather than go back for my third pull. In my head I went through all the alibis I knew—appendicitis, death in the family, a dentist's appointment. Grandpa wouldn't have let me get away with any of them. Though by then he must have been dreading our turn as much as I was.

With the boat loaded at 4,500, I felt a small energy surge from the horses. They still pulled in an uncoordinated way, but at least they pulled the full distance on the first try.

After that, the elimination started. Not that anyone was put out on the 5,500-pound pull. But it was plain to see Max Smith's horses were beginning to struggle, and Rose's young team, for all its bulk, started to strain, too.

"Ole Rose'll drop out before he risks stickin' them horses," Grandpa said.

Fielding still looked like the contest was pure

entertainment for him. Summers's team looked keen, but Kinghorn's team worried Grandpa more. The solemn-faced horses driven by the sad-eyed banjo player still could flat run away with the boat.

Scourman, it was obvious to everyone, was no teamster. But somebody had trained the Shire team beautifully, and when ordered to pull, they pulled. The crowd had turned off a bit to Scourman's rough manner, but it still loved the showy team.

On that pull, Maggie and Tom came to life, like they woke up and realized they were in a contest. They pulled now with their hearts in it and with such precision, the crowd gave us a rousing, if surprised, hand. When I returned to my place, Fielding looked over and grinned, Uncle Chatty gave me a thumbs-up sign. Grandpa rubbed his palms together and said, *"Now* we're agoin'! Shame on ya, horses, givin' a wore-out ole heart a scare like 'at!" I slumped against the fence, weak with relief.

I caught Buck Scourman looking at me. It was a steely, malevolent look. Grandpa saw it, too.

"He's sa goldurned foul-tempered, I thought he'd git hisself eliminated by now. But he's savvier'n I thought."

"Ya know he wants to hit er cuss them horses,"

Old Man Boyd put in. I thought Boyd didn't have any room to talk—until that last pull, he'd been cussing Maggie and Tom blue. But he'd done it quietly.

In Intermountain Horse Pullers Association contests, contestants aren't allowed to slap their horses with the reins or let their hookers urge the horse in any way. And judges can throw out contestants for swearing at their horses. Every try, Scourman gathered his lines in his fists and looked about ready to slap the horses, but always he managed to remember the rule and restrain himself. He'd cussed his hookers in the vilest way, but it was under his breath. To the horses, he restricted himself to mean insults. "Snivelin' nags," he'd mutter as he drove them to the boat.

Summers had trouble on the next pull. The Utah teamster in the bright red shirt had to bark "JENNY! JENNY!" to make his horses lean into the 6,500 load. But they pulled it on their second try.

It was obvious Max Smith couldn't hold on much longer, even though his Blackfoot fans were squeezing their fists and holding their breaths to help.

"Smith, he's new, and ain't usin' them horses ta their capacity," Grandpa said, "but he's a fine sport—hope he stays in pullin'."

Thane Kinghorn solemnly gathered up his lines in his thin, banjo-strumming fingers and moved to the boat. The hookers hooked, and the boat sped off only slightly slower than when it had 3,500 pounds on it. As Kinghorn passed us Grandpa called to him, "Ya got a awful fine team there."

"I'm plumb tickled with 'em," Kinghorn replied. Deep eyebags and drooping jowls made him look like a troubled hound dog.

"Looky here. Mebbe ya wrote Bud Rose off too soon," Old Man Boyd observed. The gray and roan team were up again, and this time they hit that load right and pulled it smoothly.

The bulky dark figure of Scourman moved to the boat. He had no smile for the crowd now—there was only fierce rivalry on his face.

"GIT UP!" he shouted and the horses lowered their heads and tromped forward. The flag flew out of the ground. When the big Shires passed us on their way back, Tom swiveled his head, peered around his blinders with a curious eye, and snorted.

I hoped Maggie and Tom's strong pull hadn't been an isolated, lucky try. But Grandpa and Old Man Boyd had scarcely put the hooks in place and jumped backward before Tom and Mag shoved forward as a solid gray block. From the

corner of my eye I saw a red flame leap up behind me.

Excitement crept into the announcer's voice.
"A nice pull for Andy Pendrey, our twelve-
year-old contestant from Dove Valley. Look out,
those Percherons are hot now!"

Summers decided to increase by 500 pounds
this time, probably because his team had been
balky the previous try. When the Utah teamster
moved his horses into position this time, they
were ready to work. Seconds later the flag, match-
ing his shirt, jumped into the air.

Max Smith could only pull the load six feet on
his first try, three feet on his second. His hookers
unhooked the team, and the announcer specu-
lated the hometown contestant might be back in
a few minutes for another try. But Smith shook
his head as he passed us and said, "I'm out."

For the first time, Kinghorn's solemn team
strained. The rough-coated horses managed to
pull the load, but they looked awkward and out
of harmony.

"Ain't that a surprise?" Grandpa said. "I might
be refiggerin' muh favorites. Them two've purti
near reached their limit."

Laron Fielding sauntered to the boat, grinning
behind his big brown geldings. But his voice was
urgent when he called "BIIIIILLLLL, BIIIIL-

LLL?" The horses dug in their hooves and threw their shoulders into the load. The flag didn't fly up this time. Slowly it relinquished its hold on the ground and dragged after the puffing horses.

Rose tried. His horses pulled only seven feet. He asked the big gray and roan to try again, and this time they pulled only four feet. Rose's crew unhooked and Rose walked the horses back to the gate. He would try again later after everyone else's turn.

Scourman's Shires trotted to the sled, looking fresh and ready to work. The applause was small now. Scourman settled his bulk onto the sled, pushed his heels against its footboard, and stiffened his elbows.

"GIT!" he rasped. Grandpa winced at his voice, but the willing horses charged forward and popped out the flag.

It was my turn. I noticed from the corner of my eye the Dove Valley folks were trying to lift the GOOD LUCK, ANDY banner and hold it aloft. But children were getting tangled in it, and a man carrying a tray of snow cones to his seat managed to get draped with a corner.

There was cheering as I approached the boat, and it wasn't only from the Dove Valley rooters.

I was moving them into position when Tom

began sidestepping, until he faced back toward the gate.

"This ain't no time fer your pranks," Grandpa scolded him.

"Eldro, he's lookin' at them Shires," Old Man Boyd said. "Wants ta make sure they're watchin'."

Grandpa and Old Man Boyd connected the doubletree and hopped out of the way. The excitement had cured their creaky backs.

Maggie and Tom thrust their weight against the boat's, and, with military precision, marched forward with their load. The flag leaped up.

Rose came back for another try, but could only pull seven feet again. The crowd gave him a nice hand. "Two out," Grandpa said, "and we're still in."

I guess Dell Summers wanted to keep the contest lively, because he ordered 1,000 pounds added. Usually 8,000 to 8,500 won the middleweight division. I didn't know if Maggie and Tom could pull 8,000 pounds. But I was pleased with how they'd done. The worst I could get now was fifth—I might even get fourth and be in the money! And best of all, Maggie and Tom had looked like real pullers.

Dell Summers wiped his forehead with his red shirtsleeve, ran a hand through his skimpy hair,

and replaced his cap. Then his hookers picked
up the doubletree and walked to the sled.

"Jennnnny! JENNNNNY!!" Summers bal-
anced over the edge of the boat. The crowd was
silent. The horses grunted. Foam dripped from
their mouths as they inched forward, and water
ran off their necks. It looked for a moment like
they would stop before they pulled up the flag,
but Summers pleaded, "JENNNNNNNNY!" and
slowly, the flag eased out of the dust and flopped
over on its side.

Most people in the stands were on their feet,
waving programs and whistling.

"That's a fine team," Grandpa said. "I knowed
they had it in 'em—don't know why they struggled on that one pull."

The long-faced Kinghorn moved to the boat.
"He can't do it," Grandpa predicted. "He coulda
did seventy-five hundred, but he can't do eight."

I wasn't so sure. Kinghorn's team had been
running away with the loads until that last pull.
And Summers's horses had proved a team could
come back after a bad pull.

With a forlorn expression, Kinghorn asked his
horses to pull. The pair heaved ahead, lay back
their ears, and stumbled. Like they didn't know
how to pull together on a load that was heavy for

them. They stopped. Officials measured. It was seven and a half feet.

Kinghorn shook his head at his crew—he was declining another pull, and climbed off the boat. He handed the lines to one of his hookers, lifted his hat to the crowd, smiled!—and walked off beside the horses, patting one on its rump. He could still finish in the money, depending on how far the rest of us pulled.

Fielding, still grinning, was up next. He settled onto the sled and called, "BILLLLLL? BBBBBI-IIIIIILLLLL!" His browns lowered their heads, clawed in the dust, and drove forward. They strained forward with determination, but the flag remained planted. Officials measured nine and a half feet. Fielding snapped his fingers—the crowd moaned. He would try again later.

Scourman, spitting orders to his crew, swaggered up. His brows locked his face in a scowl. He crouched on the sled, jiggling the reins. "NOW!" he ordered.

His crew jumped aside. "HYYYYAAAAAHH-HHHHH!" he cried.

I think if Scourman's horses could have seen his face and the ugliness on it, they wouldn't have pulled. But well-mannered team that they were, they heaved forward on orders. Greenish foam oozed from their bits, sweat frothed over their rumps and shoulders, and Scourman's bone-chilling whoop still sliced the air. Then the flag was yanked up.

There was almost no applause. Even the beauty and courage of the Shire team couldn't make the crowd forgive the horridness of Scourman. A few of the teamsters clapped politely, but Grandpa and Old Man Boyd didn't. As we passed Scourman and his crew returning, there was silence between us, except for the cavernous gasps of the black horses.

Grandpa gave me no last-minute instructions about the pull. The excitement and concentration were beginning to make me feel heavy and thickheaded. I don't know if I could have understood advice. Grandpa did say something to our horses.

"Shires didn't build America—Percherons did!" Then he and Old Man Boyd slipped the hooks into place.

I was a robot frozen in place on the stone-boat. I don't remember what I called out to the horses. I hoped my hands, numb from clenching, sent them a message of encouragement. I stared ahead as the horses' heads disappeared into their chests, their shoulders began to bulge with effort, and their rump muscles swelled and turned white with lather. Grandpa yelled, "They done it!"

Above me in the stands the GOOD LUCK, ANDY banner billowed. I stared at the bleachers. From the first row to the top bleacher, people were on their feet yelling and whistling. It was for me.

Fielding came back for another try. He'd come so close before, I hoped he could do it this time. But his team pulled only four and a half feet. Grandpa slapped me.

"We're in the top three! Hot dang!"

CHAPTER 17

There were three of us left. Maggie and Tom, in the company of two strong teams, had survived. Dell Summers, gesturing with his red-sleeved arm, talked with a fair official. A moment later the white truck drove up and the fair crew threw five 100-pound sacks of gravel onto the boat.

"Competing for the title today in this exciting middleweight contest," the announcer called, "are Dell Summers from Bountiful, Utah, Buck Scourman from Burley, Idaho, and Andy Pendrey, our fine twelve-year-old competitor from Dove Valley, Idaho. They're lined up and ready to go for the eighty-five-hundred-pound pull."

"Summers's team looked a little tired, but I think they can do it," Grandpa said. "Summers pulled eighty-five hundred to win first last year."

A frown deepened the creases on his face.

"Don't *you* worry none, Andy. Ya done plumb

good awready. Just make a good try." Grandpa's reassurance betrayed he didn't think Maggie and Tom could pull it. But like him, I was satisfied with our showing. For years I'd dreamed of winning glory for myself at the fair. Now it seemed enough that we'd done a good job.

Summers looked sober as he picked up his lines and moved into position. His crew slipped in the hooks, jumped aside, and Summers's voice pleaded "JEEEEENNNNNNY!" His horses strained, pawed dust, then dug in deep and sent dirt clods flying. Summers shook his head. The team had pulled four and a half feet.

"Unhook," he called to his hookers. "We ain't trying again. They're too tired."

I suppose Summers felt the other two teams wouldn't pull very far either. With luck he might still finish in first place.

But Scourman's horses trotted to the boat, pulled against their bits, and danced while the hookers backed them to the stoneboat.

"Ya gotta hand it to 'em," Wellington said. "Them two're fresh as July peaches."

"We'll see," said Grandpa. I think even more than wanting us to win, Grandpa wanted Scourman to lose.

Scourman gave his earsplitting whoop and the team threw their weight into the load. Slowly, the sled eased forward. It was a leaden, suspenseful pull, and I thought the blacks would stop before they uprooted the flag, but they didn't. The flag twitched, then crept out of the earth. There was scattered applause.

I moved to the boat with Maggie and Tom. Despite my excitement, my stomach was quiet. The spectators whistled, cheered, and stomped their feet. Instead of the lazy team I'd started with that day, I now held two snorting horses with perked ears, quivering nostrils, and tensed muscles. Grandpa and Wellington Boyd knew they needed to hop after they hooked me up.

All afternoon I'd been aware of the crowd in the bleachers, the screams from the midway rides, the announcer and his comments, the other teams lined up by the fence. Now the horses took my whole attention. This time the message came from them to me, carried along lines connecting their heads to my hands.

"Pull!" the message said and I pulled with them. I squeezed shut my eyes, ground my teeth, and clenched my hands until the flesh tingled. For a couple of seconds after I called, "Maggie! Tom!" it seemed like the sled didn't move. Then I felt a rolling surge under me.

"Hot dang! They done it! Hot dang! They done it!" Grandpa yelled. I opened my eyes and blinked. The GOOD LUCK, ANDY banner was crumpled on a bleacher. Its holders were on their feet, jumping and hugging each other. The announcer was babbling "Only twelve years old! Think of it!" I was grinning so hard I worried my face would split.

By the gate, Grandpa laid down the hitching tree. He straightened up and looked at me. Tears were seeping down the crooked ruts of his face.

"Thank ya, Andy," he whispered. "Thank ya fer this day. I'm a ole man. I didn't think I had it left in me ta feel what I feel taday."

He pressed my elbow. "Them horses, and you, Andy, I never wanted ta git mixed up with none o' ya. I never knowed when Linden would change 'is mind and want ya back home. Then like Josie and your dad, you'd be gone. When Maggie and Tom was little, and you was afeedin' Tom, I said ta muhself, 'Eldro, don't git mixed up in this—ya'll git your heart broke.' But look at me now . . ." He dug a blue handkerchief from his overalls and mopped his cheeks, then honked his nose and wiped it. Blinking tears, he turned to watch the fair crew loading the stoneboat.

At five sacks the crew kept going. Six, seven, eight, nine, ten!

Ten! Scourman was now in the number one place—had he ordered 1,000 pounds added? At these heavy weights, teamsters always increased by 500.

"Don't he care nothin' about them horses?" Grandpa scolded.

"Grandpa, did Maggie and Tom have trouble with that last pull? I wasn't watching."

"They fought fer it purty hard."

"Maybe I should stop now. They're young."

"Might do. Let's watch and see how Scourman's blacks pull. They outweigh your team by four hundred pounds. If they get stuck . . ."

The Shires did not trot now. They trudged to the sled, heads down—their earlier fire used up.

Scourman arranged himself on the sled, hunched his shoulders, and blew out through bared teeth, "Now!" His hookers jumped back, Scourman howled, "HYYYYYAAAAAHHHH!" and the big tired blacks began to pull.

They dug footholds, churned up dirt clods, staggered, then struggled forward. Lather foamed on their necks and shoulders. They trembled with fatigue and drank air in mountainous gulps. It wasn't thrilling to watch them now. Before, they'd been power and courage. Now they were worry and strain.

Inch by inch they heaved ahead, and before they stopped, the flag had fallen on its side.

"Is ninety-five hundred a fair record?" Fielding asked Grandpa.

"Nope. Somebody done it before, but only once er twice."

I'd seen what the pull had done to the Shires. I wouldn't ask that of my team. I might injure them, or sour them on pulling forever. Grandpa caught my eye. I shook my head. Grandpa nodded, slowly. He didn't care about first place, but he sure wanted to lick Scourman. Still, I'd made Maggie and Tom a promise that day in the timber—that I'd never ask a too-hard thing of them again, and I didn't lie to my horses.

Grandpa and Wellington Boyd picked up the doubletree so we could return to the waiting area and unhitch. Tom didn't seem to understand where we were headed. He tried to walk to the stoneboat. I felt silly—walking my team in a circle. Giggles floated from the grandstand. "Tom!" I ordered. He marched off in the opposite way. I went in another circle while Tom swiveled his head. He was giving me a dirty look.

"*He* ain't ready ta quit," Grandpa said.

"He's still got somethin' ta prove," Old Man Boyd called.

I gave him his head. When the spectators saw us moving to the boat, they leaped to their feet and cheered. Then they sat down, silent as owls.

"Tom," I said as I eased myself into place, "you asked for this yourself. So give it your best."

Grandpa was stooped over the hooks. As he jumped aside, I saw his face, as hopeful as a kid's. I called again, "Your *best!*"

For a moment, I thought the boat was anchored in place. Then it began to sway. I looked at Maggie and Tom and they were swaying—left, right, left, right. Their muscles were taut, their shoulders bulged. Earth clods flew past my face. Left, right, grinding forward. Maggie and Tom moved with such unity that once the sled began to roll, I knew they'd drag it the full ten feet. It was the most enjoyable pull of the day for me, watching Maggie's and Tom's rock-solid power used in perfect harmony.

The crowd was wild. The announcer couldn't be heard over the thunder of their cries. Even first-time spectators knew they'd seen a great pulling team.

"Did ya see 'em?" Grandpa hollered. "They was one mind in two horses!"

"Course!" Old Man Boyd said. "They're twins, ain't they? I awwus told ya twins has got somethin' real special."

Grandpa shot Old Man Boyd a fierce look and

opened his mouth to protest. But a fair truck pulled up then, carrying more sand.

"Scourman think he kin put 'is team through another pull?"

"Eldro, he don't care nothin' about that team. He just wants ta show up your boy."

The crew loaded on 500 more pounds. It was getting hard to find a place for sacks on the loaded red, white, and blue stoneboat.

As he passed us, Scourman narrowed his eyes and grimaced. He approached the sled. A few spectators did something I'd never heard at a pulling contest. Booed.

Scourman crouched on the sled, working his mouth and sliding his fingers up and down on the reins.

The sandy-haired kid and Harrop hooked. Scourman let go with an eagle scream. And then, forgetting himself, he lifted the reins and cracked them down on the horse's flanks. The other teamsters smiled. Scourman had disqualified himself.

Scourman didn't realize his mistake immediately and continued his banshee cry. The Shires had jumped when Scourman hit them, but made no attempt to push forward. They were through working for him.

An official leaned over the sled and spoke to Scourman. Scourman leaped off, waving clenched fists, and came toward the huddle of officials. I think he might have hit someone, but the boos and yells from the stands finally drove him off the field.

Roland Harrop hung his head as he unhooked the doubletree. The sandy-haired kid, I noticed, was grinning. Laron Fielding sprinted over and gathered up the lines Scourman had left on the ground and walked the Shires to the gate.

I wanted to see how my horses would do on the 10,000-pound load. After their last pull, I didn't worry about them hurting themselves. If they decided not to pull at all, that would be all right, but I wanted to give them a chance. Laron Fielding called to me, "I figger it'll be a record if ya pull this." Grandpa, Old Man Boyd, and I walked to the boat.

Grandpa and Wellington Boyd looked nervous, the horses looked anxious. The stadium was hushed. I didn't know what to call to Maggie and Tom for encouragement. So I sang, in a quiet voice.

"I ain't got no mother, I ain't got no mother . . ."

Tom's ears perked, then wiggled and pointed back toward me. Mag's ears wiggled toward Tom. Then, with a unified motion, the horses tucked themselves into steel-gray boulders and rolled forward.

Five hundred more pounds made it harder. They dug in, muscles popping, shoulders swollen, hearts thumping against their lathered hides. They pulled with one mind, but they were depending on Maggie's greater strength. Her forelegs scrambled in the dirt like she was in quicksand, and she got down and fought so hard her belly scraped the ground. You couldn't have thrown a baby's hat under her.

"I'm a poor lonesome cowboy, a poor lonesome cowboy . . ."

I don't think they heard. They were lost in concentration and exertion. The lines in my hand quivered from the horses' strain. I felt the boat begin to rock. And then move ahead.

They had to grapple for every step. But I knew they wouldn't quit until I said it was okay.

"And a long way from home."

I glanced behind me. The flag was beginning to waver. Then it teetered and toppled.

I swung from the boat and ran to my horses. I hugged them around their necks and told them thanks and I love you and a lot of foolish things, too.

Grandpa was leaning against Maggie and tears were streaming down his leathered face. Old

Man Boyd was turned away, blowing his nose.

I remembered something. "Unhook me!" I ordered.

I gathered up my lines, jumped on the doubletree, and rode to the stands.

The crowd had spilled unevenly onto the front of the grandstand. People were leaning on the fence and each other, waving and cheering. When I rode by, the place exploded with a roar. Loretta Hodges was hanging on the fence, supported by her husband, her hair in her eyes, her face collapsed with weeping. Bobby was jumping and whistling through his fingers.

I returned to Grandpa. Old Man Boyd sniffled, "I awwus knowed they was special." Grandpa wiped his dripping nose and choked. "That's a lie! Ya woulda let one of 'em die if I hadn'ta straightened ya out!"

"I wouldn'ta let 'im die," Boyd sniffed.

Grandpa smacked Old Man Boyd on the arm. Old Man Boyd gave Grandpa a poke in the ribs. Grandpa grabbed Old Man Boyd by the elbow and swung him in a circle. Old Man Boyd crossed his arms in front of him and do-si-doed around Grandpa.

Laron Fielding caught me up in his arms and hugged me. Someone with a slow voice spoke my

name. It was Kinghorn, wearing his woebegone
face.

"An-dy, I'm plumb tick-led for ya. I never had
. . . a better time . . . than watchin' ya today." He
shook my hand forlornly.

By now people in the stands had pushed past
the uniformed fair policemen and were streaming onto the field. The first of them had reached
Maggie and Tom and were stroking them rever-
ently.

I saw Dad striding across the field, wiping sweat
off his forehead. His usually neat hair was
mussed.

"Son." He hugged my shoulders. "Good job!"
He swiveled his head around to see what was
making a sound like chickens. It was Grandpa,
Wellington Boyd, and Uncle Chatty.

"I've never seen the old man so pleased." Dad
said it with a laugh, but the corners of his
mouth drooped. He turned back to me. His
eyes rested on my face. "You're tall, Andy. I noticed that today. From the bleachers, you looked
so big." He paused. "Before I know it, you'll be
grown."

"Dad." I think he was going to ask me to come
home. Hadn't I hoped he'd someday see I was
just as important as his job? But now it felt wrong.

Now I wanted to stay in Dove Valley with Grandpa.

I felt clumsy reaching for his hand to shake, but I did it. "Dad. Thanks for coming," I said. I meant it. From the corner of my eye I'd spotted Mr. Reynolds, the forest supervisor.

I turned to go, and ran smack into Grandpa. I didn't know how long he'd been there.

"Grandpa!"

"Ya got a hunnert people waitin' ta see ya! Git over there!" Grandpa and Dad gazed at each other. Then Grandpa's brows dove together and he dropped his head and stared at his scuffed old work boots.

"Andy!" Mr. Reynolds called. "This is my wife, Marge. We can't tell you what a thrilling afternoon this has been for us. *Congratulations!*" He wrung my hand until I thought it'd fall off.

For another fifteen minutes it went like that—people I knew and people I never saw before came by and pumped my hand and told me how they liked my horses. When I finally got a chance to sit down and take a drink, my arm was so tired I barely could lift my canteen.

The announcer pleaded for people to return to their seats for the heavyweight contest. Presently, six teams paraded past the stands. Spectators applauded, but only lightly. It was obvious the crowd had worn itself out on the middleweight competition.

Now my part was over, I could enjoy the rest of the afternoon. Grandpa and Wellington Boyd had put Maggie and Tom away and given them oats and a drink. The three of us sat on a pickup with Kinghorn to trade opinions about the heavyweight teams.

It was a subdued but capable contest. The winner, George Vernon, pulled 8,500 with a pretty team of geldings—one bay, one white.

As Vernon rode to the stands to collect his trophy, Grandpa turned to me.

"I got an idee." He motioned for me to follow, away from the others. "I been thinkin'—about the future."

His eye held a gleam. Next month the National Championship Pulling Horse Contest would be held in Salt Lake City—was he going to suggest we go to it? Or was he scheming a barn or new equipment for Maggie and Tom? Or did he want to talk ways we might spend the prize money?

He leaned close.

"Let's git us a dog."

"A dog?!"

"Shhh! Well, not a dog. A pup."

I gazed at him. "Huh?"

"Horses is fine. But they live outside. Ain't part

o' the household, follerin' ever'where, gittin' un-
derfoot."

"Sure. That'd be great."

"And some chickens? Few ole clucks ta give us
eggs? I awwus liked gatherin' eggs when I was a
kid."

"Yeah. Okay."

"Yessir," he smiled, "that'd be just right. A pup
dog and a few ole chickabiddies. Holy Jumped-
up Moses! Just like a real family."